TALL, DARK, AND DEADLY

The door drove her back with such force that she landed on her back. By the time she managed to sit up, the man was inside, the door closed, and he was pointing a gun at her.

"Where are they?" he asked. He was a tall man with dark hair, dark eyes, and dark skin. She'd never seen him before and yet, there was something vaguely familiar about him.

"Where's who?"

"Don't play with me, lady," the man said. "I'm in no mood."

The man cocked the hammer on his gun and jabbed it toward Sam.

"Are they upstairs?"

"Mister," Sam said, "you don't want to do this. You don't—"

"Don't tell me what I want!"

Sam looked over at her gun, which was on the floor in the middle of the entry foyer. The man with the gun in his hand looked over there as well. He flexed his hand on the butt of his gun and shuffled his feet nervously.

"Don't think about it," he said. "You'll never make it."

DON'T MISS THESE
ALL-ACTION WESTERN SERIES
FROM THE BERKLEY PUBLISHING GROUP

THE GUNSMITH by J. R. Roberts
Clint Adams was a legend among lawmen, outlaws, and ladies.
They called him . . . the Gunsmith.

LONGARM by Tabor Evans
The popular long-running series about U.S. Deputy Marshal
Long—his life, his loves, his fight for justice.

SLOCUM by Jake Logan
Today's longest-running action Western. John Slocum rides
a deadly trail of hot blood and cold steel.

BUSHWHACKERS by B. J. Lanagan
An action-packed series by the creators of Longarm! The
rousing adventures of the most brutal gang of cutthroats ever
assembled—Quantrill's Raiders.

DIAMONDBACK by Guy Brewer
Dex Yancey is Diamondback, a southern gentleman turned
con man when his brother cheats him out of the family for-
tune. Ladies love him. Gamblers hate him. But nobody pulls
one over on Dex . . .

WILDGUN by Jack Hanson
Will Barlow's continuing search for his daughter, kidnapped
by the Blackfeet Indians who slaughtered the rest of his family.

THE GUNSMITH

BARNUM AND BULLETS

J. R. ROBERTS

JOVE BOOKS, NEW YORK

BARNUM AND BULLETS

A Jove Book / published by arrangement with
the author

PRINTING HISTORY
Jove edition / September 2000

The Penguin Putnam Inc. World Wide Web site address is
http://www.penguinputnam.com

ISBN: 0-515-12908-9

A JOVE BOOK®
Jove Books are published by The Berkley Publishing Group,
a division of Penguin Putnam Inc.,
375 Hudson Street, New York, New York 10014.
JOVE and the "J" design
are trademarks belonging to Penguin Putnam Inc.

PRINTED IN THE UNITED STATES OF AMERICA

10 9 8 7 6 5 4 3 2 1

PROLOGUE

The main reason for Clint Adams's visit to New York City was his continued depression over not being able to find a horse to replace his trusted black gelding, Duke, who had been put out to pasture earlier that year. In an attempt to combat his depression he took in every kind of entertainment possible: sporting events, the theater, curiosity shows, and even the circus. In particular, he went to the recently erected Madison Square Garden to see P. T. Barnum's Circus.

Madison Square Garden had recently been renovated, as J. P. Morgan, Andrew Carnegie, James Stillman and W. W. Astor pooled their resources, bought it and hired famed architect Standford White to design a new building. It took thousands of men and eleven months—not to mention $1.5 million—but one of the largest and finest public entertainment halls finally opened its doors to

1

the likes of Buffalo Bill Cody's Wild West Show and P. T. Barnum's Circus.

However, Clint did not attend the circus alone. He went in the company of a lovely lady he had met only two days after arriving in New York. Her name was Felicity Parker. She was from Boston and had come to New York "on holiday," she explained. They were staying at the same hotel and had met in the crowded hotel dining room, where Clint asked if he would be allowed to share her table. Thereafter, they shared much more than a table.

As they approached Madison Square Garden, Clint marveled at the structure. He had seen many odd things happen to New York over the years from visit to visit, not the least of which was a train—an elevated train— built above ground, and a subway, which was a train that ran below ground. The Garden, as it was called, was New York's newest attraction.

As they stood in line to buy their tickets, Felicity said, "I understand P. T. Barnum is supposed to be a genius."

"A genius at flimflamming the public."

"You mean he cheats the public?"

"I mean he manages to give the public what they want without really giving it to them," Clint said. "He's sort of a magician when it comes to that."

She looked at him and said, "You sound as if you know him?"

"Well . . . we've met."

She grabbed his arm.

"You've met P. T. Barnum?"

"It was a while ago," Clint said, "while he was on the road."

"Oh, Clint, you have to tell me about it," she said, excitedly. "You have to."

"Well, we're going in to see the show, Felicity."

"Can you tell me about it afterward?"

"Uh, sure I can," he said. "Of course, but it's not—"

"And why are we paying to get in if you know him so well?"

"Well," Clint said, "I didn't say I knew him well . . . in fact, I didn't even say that we were friends."

"You mean you're not?"

"You know, Felicity," he said, "let's see the show and then I'll take you to dinner and it will all come out in the telling."

"I can't wait!"

Clint hadn't thought about Phineas T. Barnum in quite a while . . .

PART ONE

PART ONE.

ONE

When Clint rode into Fort Hays he was looking forward to seeing his friend Bat Masterson. At this point, he had no idea that General George Armstrong Custer was commanding Fort Hays, or that his friend Bat Masterson would not be able to meet him there after all. Buffalo hunting with Bat would have to wait for another time.

But he didn't know that. He was anxious to see his friend and catch up on what he'd been up to since the last time they had both seen each other in the company of their other friend, Wyatt Earp.

He entered the fort through the front gate, stopping to identify himself and be passed by the sentry. From there he rode into town and went directly to the livery stable before continuing in to the Hays House Hotel, where he and Bat were supposed to meet up. That was when he found out that Bat would not be coming.

The Hays House Hotel was one of the few buildings in town that did not look as if it were going to fall down. Most of the buildings were ramshackle huts and shacks and shanties, some covered by canvas. It was a rowdy place, to say the least. As Clint approached the hotel he heard so much shooting from another part of town that it sounded like firecrackers going off.

"Your key, sir," the clerk said to him when he checked in, "and you already have a message."

The clerk handed Clint the telegraph message that had been waiting there for him since the day before.

It was from Bat and read: CAN'T MAKE IT. SOME-THING CAME UP. SHOOT ONE FOR ME. BAT.

"Fine," Clint said, crumpling the message and stuffing it into his pocket.

"A problem, sir?" the clerk asked.

"Nothing you can help me with, I'm afraid," Clint said. "The friend I was supposed to be meeting here is not coming."

"That's too bad," the clerk said. "Perhaps you'll find something in town to amuse you, anyway."

"Something," Clint said, picking up his rifle and sad-dlebags, "or some*one*. You can bet I'll be looking."

He was turning to start up to his room but was dis-tracted when a group of men came walking into the ho-tel, talking loudly among themselves as if no one else was around.

". . . can't wait to get out there," one of them was saying. "I've heard they're incredible."

"They are," another man said. "I've seen them. Sometimes you find one or two, but when you find a large herd it's almost like looking over a sea of them."

There were easily half a dozen men, and they were obviously discussing buffalo hunting. Apparently, they were already registered at the hotel because they went directly to the stairs and started up. Clint deliberately remained at the desk so he wouldn't have to use the stairs at the same time as the loud group.

"I got a message that P. T. is coming," another loud voiced called. The last man in line called out to the first as they filed up the stairs.

"He is," the lead man said. "Getting tired of being retired, I think, and he's old friends with the commander here. He'll be along some time in the next few days."

"I've got to see ol' P. T. with a buffalo gun," another man said as they reached the top of the stairs. "He's gonna have to shoot 'em, because he won't be able to flimflam them—"

The voices faded out as the men walked down the hall. Clint turned and looked at the desk clerk.

"A group from the East," the man explained. "Here to hunt buffalo."

"So I gathered," Clint said. "Are they always that loud?"

"I'm afraid so."

Clint looked down at his key.

"Is my room anywhere near theirs?"

"I managed to put most of them at one end of the hotel," the man said. "If you like, I can make sure you're at the other end—in the back?"

Clint handed back his key and said, "Do it."

"Yes, sir."

The clerk took the key and exchanged it for another.

"Thanks," Clint said, accepting the key. "How many of them are there, anyway?"

"Ten," the clerk said, "and it sounded as if they were expecting another."

"Yes, it did," Clint said, unhappily, "didn't it?"

TWO

Clint was having second thoughts about staying in Fort Hays as the noise made by the buffalo-hunting easterners filtered down to his end of the floor, joining with the sound of shots from outside. He thought about going down to ask them to be quiet but decided that would only result in getting himself even more annoyed. Instead, he left the hotel in search of a meal. He hoped that the oddly named "P. T." who they were waiting for would not be someone who would add to the din.

He found a small café a few blocks from the hotel and indulged himself with a huge steak for lunch. He'd been on the trail for some time and was tired of eating beef jerky and beans—although good, strong trail coffee was something he never tired of and could hardly get when off the trail. Sometimes that kind of coffee had to be strong enough to hold you up in the saddle.

After his meal he walked back to the hotel, on several occasions having to move out of the way to keep from either being run over by a horse or buckboard or bumped into by men arguing. Tempers seemed to be high in Hays City.

When he entered the hotel, a soldier, a young corporal, was waiting in the lobby. As Clint entered, the clerk nodded, and the corporal approached him.

"Sir? Do I have the honor of addressing Clint Adams?"

"You do, Corporal," Clint said. "What is this about?"

"My commanding officer would like you to accompany me to his office, sir," the soldier said.

"What's this about, soldier?"

"I don't know, sir," the man said. "I was just sent to fetch you."

"Those were your orders?" Clint asked. "To fetch me?"

"No, sir," the corporal said. "My orders were to invite you to come to the fort to talk with the colonel."

"And just who is your commanding officer, Corporal?"

"Colonel George Armstrong Custer, sir."

"Custer," Clint said. The fair-haired boy of the Seventh Cavalry. Custer's rise through the ranks was almost legendary. If Clint remembered correctly, Custer was barely thirty years old. He thought it might be interesting to meet the man.

"All right, Corporal," he said. "I'll come with you to meet your commanding officer."

"Thank you, sir."

"I really don't have all that much of anything else to do, anyway, so lead on."

"Yes, sir."

The soldier went out the front door with Clint in tow.

"Corporal?"

"Yes, sir?"

"You got a civilian lawman here?"

"Yes, sir, a sheriff."

"What's his name?"

"Latimer."

There were gunshots down the street, just then.

"There seems to be a lot of shooting in this town."

"Yes, sir," the soldier said. "Seems to be the way people want to solve their differences."

"Doesn't the sheriff do anything about it?"

"I guess," the corporal said. "Does seem, though, that the undertaker does more about it than the sheriff."

"Like what?"

"Like buryin' them up on Boot Hill."

"Where?"

"Boot Hill," the corporal said. "The cemetery."

"Who named it Boot Hill?"

"Don't rightly know," the man said. "That's just what people around here call it."

"I see."

They passed through the rear gate from Hays City into Fort Hays, and it suddenly seemed much calmer.

"Quieter here."

"The colonel rules with a bit more authority here than the sheriff does in town," the corporal said.

"That so? Makes liberal use of the stockade?"

"I guess you could call it that."

"What else would you call it but the stockade?"

"Well . . . it ain't a stockade, exactly."

"What is it, then?"

"More like . . . a hole in the ground."

"What?"

"He had this hole dug in the ground and, for a while, whenever a man would try to desert, he'd end up in that hole."

"A hole? In the ground?"

"Yes, sir."

"What kind of hole."

The corporal looked back at Clint, then slowed so they could walk side by side. "You'll see it when we enter the fort," he said. "It's a twenty foot circular hole, twenty feet deep, with a roof of logs and a ladder leading down into it."

"Did you have a lot of desertions early on?"

"Some," the man said. "What with the Sioux, Cheyenne and Arapaho actin' up, lots of fellas didn't think they was gonna get to go home alive. Also, any military man acting up in town, or breaking military law, would find themselves down in that hole."

"And this hole in the ground—it cured them?"

"Sure seems to have," the corporal said.

"Uh-huh. You ever been in that hole, Corporal?"

"Me? No, sir. I don't have any desire to spend a few days in a hole in the ground, sir."

"What's your name, Corporal?"

"Hailey, sir. Corporal John Hailey."

"You sound like a smart young man, Corporal."

"I ain't that smart, sir," Hailey said, "but I learn fast."

THREE

Clint followed Corporal Hailey to the C.O.'s office and knew he was going to have to wade through an officer or two before he finally got to Custer. As promised, he saw the circular hole covered by logs, and he wondered if there was anyone down there at the moment.

As they entered the outer office he saw a lieutenant sitting at a desk, going through some paperwork. He was prepared to have to be introduced to this man and answer some questions but was surprised when the lieutenant looked up at him and said, "Go right in, sir. The colonel is waiting."

"Well," Clint said, "he must have been pretty sure I'd come."

"He was," the lieutenant said, without looking up. "That's all, Corporal."

"Yes, sir."

15

"Thanks for seeing me over here, Corporal."

"Yes, sir," Hailey said. "Just doin' my job."

He saluted. Clint was unsure who the salute was for, because he didn't see the lieutenant return it.

"Go right in," the lieutenant said, again.

"Thanks."

Clint went to the door, considered knocking on it, but then decided that if he was supposed to go right in, he would.

"Mr. Adams?" the man behind the desk asked.

"That's right."

"Excellent!"

Custer stood and came around the desk. He didn't look like any colonel—or officer—Clint had ever seen before. He was wearing regulation army pants, but instead of a regulation tunic he had on a buckskin jacket. Also, his blond hair was long and flowing, and while long hair was not unusual in the West, it was usually plainsmen who wore it that way, not Army officers. He also had a very well cared for beard and mustache, which did little to hide the fact that he was very young to be a colonel—younger, even, then the lieutenant sitting outside the door, which may have explained that officer's attitude.

Custer took Clint's hand and shook it enthusiastically.

"I took the liberty of having some coffee brought in," he said, indicating the ornate pot that sat on his desk. Next to it were two china cups. "I had my wife bring it in. The china was her idea."

"I see."

"Would you care for a cup?"

"I wouldn't want Mrs. Custer's kindness to go to waste," Clint said.

"My wife's name is Libby," Custer said as he poured two cups of coffee. "You'll be meeting her later. She'll be accompanying us."

"Accompanying us?" Clint asked, accepting the cup. "I don't understand. Accompanying us where?"

"On the hunt."

"What hunt?"

"Forgive me," Custer said. Instead of sitting behind his desk he simply propped one hip on it. "I'm getting way ahead of myself. Allow me to explain."

Clint remained silent so the man could do so.

"I have some visiting dignitaries coming into town with the intention of doing some buffalo hunting. I, uh, do have something of a reputation for buffalo hunting—as, I understand, you do."

"I've done some."

"In company with Wyatt Earp and Bat Masterson, I understand."

"Sometimes, yes."

"I would like you to hunt with us, sir."

It was not Clint's immediate reaction to accept, even though he had come to Hays City to hunt with Bat.

"That's a very kind offer, Colonel," Clint said. "May I ask who these visiting dignitaries are?"

"Oh, some politicians and businessmen from back East," Custer said. "I understand that one of them—a man named K. C. Barker—is the mayor of Detroit, Michigan."

"I see."

"But there's another man coming who is a friend of mine, who will be hunting with them," Custer said. "I would very much like to make sure he enjoys himself, and I think meeting you would almost ensure that."

"I'm flattered," Clint said. "Who is this man?"

"Someone you may have heard of," Custer said, "and who you might be interested in meeting. His name is Phineas T. Barnum—P. T. Barnum, for short."

Of course, Clint had heard of P. T. Barnum, the great showman. One of the men in the hotel had mentioned the name "P. T.," but Clint had not made the connection at that time.

"Barnum."

"You know the name?'

"I do," Clint said. "I've heard of his exploits in the East."

"And would you be interested in meeting him?"

"I would, indeed."

"Excellent!" Custer said, happily. "Then you'll accept my invitation?"

"I will, with pleasure, Colonel," Clint said. "Thank you."

"I'm sure you and P. T. will get on famously."

With that, Custer stood up and walked around his desk. Clint had a feeling that his afternoon coffee with the colonel was over.

"He'll be arriving in Hays City tomorrow, and I thought we'd go out the next day."

"I'll be ready."

Clint stood up and placed his cup back on the desk.

"You said Mrs. Custer will be accompanying us?"

"Yes," Custer said, "Libby will be playing hostess in our camp."

"Won't that be dangerous for her?" Clint asked. "I mean, what with the Indians—"

"I don't think there'll be a problem," Custer said.

"You see, I plan on taking at least fifty troopers with us."

"I see."

"I'll send a man with all the particulars as to when and where, Mr. Adams," Custer said. "Right now, I need to get back to work."

"I understand, Colonel. I just have one question."

"And what would that be?"

"How did you know I was here, in Hays City?"

"You made quite an impression on the sentry who passed you through the front gate," Custer explained. "He started talking about you, and the word eventually got back to me. I then sent the corporal into town to see if you were registered at the hotel and to extend to you this invitation."

"I see. I was just curious."

"I'm sure a man of your reputation is used to having it precede you."

"I'm sure you have that problem just as much as I do, Colonel," Clint said, "if not more."

"A reputation can be a cumbersome thing, some-times . . ."

"Yes, it can—"

". . . unless, of course, you intend to go into politics."

Custer laughed at his own joke and then walked Clint to the door of his office.

"I'll be seeing you soon," he said, and ushered him out.

As the door closed, the lieutenant looked up at Clint, and they locked eyes.

"He's really something, isn't he?" Clint asked.

The lieutenant looked down at his desk and said, "That's one way of putting it."

FOUR

On the way out of the C.O.'s office, Clint once again spotted the log top of the hole in the ground Custer used as a stockade. He wondered where the man would ever have come up with an idea like that, and what his superiors would think of it, if they knew.

And *did* they know?

One of the first things George Armstrong Custer had done when he arrived in Fort Hays was to have a door cut into the rear wall of his office, which would connect the office to his living quarters. When Clint Adams was gone he walked to the door and went through.

Custer's wife was Libbie—Elizabeth Clifton Bacon, before they married. She was very attractive, with a slender figure, brown hair, and blue eyes. She had been very flirtatious when they met and continued to be that way even after they married. There had been an incident where Custer worried that she might even have gone further than being flirtatious. This was one of the reasons Custer was happy for this outpost. It was also the reason she was going to be along on the hunt, so Custer wouldn't have to be wondering what she was doing back at the fort while he was away.

"Hello, dear," he said, entering the kitchen. He'd been able to follow the scent of apple pie in order to find her there.

She turned quickly, eyes flashing, and asked, "Did he agree?"

"Mr. Adams?" Custer asked. "Of course he did. I did not give him the opportunity *not* to agree."

"What is he like?" she asked, clasping her hands together. "Is he as fearsome-looking as his reputation?

"My dear," he said, "you, of all people, know how overblown a reputation can be."

"All except yours, my dear," she replied.

"Well," he said, puffing out his chest, "certain people do deserve all their notoriety."

"This will be quite exciting," she said, "meeting P. T. Barnum and Clint Adams—one a legend in the East, the other a legend in the West."

"Yes, of course," Custer said. P. T. Barnum amused him, and he did not yet know what he thought of Clint Adams, but certainly neither man impressed him as a *legend*. In truth, few legends interested George Armstrong Custer beyond himself.

"Yes, well, P. T. will be arriving tomorrow, so you can plan on going on the hunt the day after."

"Good. I'll pack a picnic lunch for you and I, as well as Mr. Barnum and Mr. Adams."

Custer chuckled. "My men won't like that much."

"Let them bring their own food," Libbie said. "I'm not packing food for fifty more people."

"I don't blame you, my dear," Custer said. "I'll be in my office for the remainder of the day."

He walked over to where she was standing in front of the stove and kissed her cheek quickly.

"Will we be going for our ride later?" Libbie asked.

"Of course, dear. I shall come and fetch you."

The Custers usually rode together in the evenings, sometimes joined by Custer's brother, Tom, and his wife, Autie.

Custer went back to his office.

Libbie turned to look at Eliza, a black servant who had been with the Custers for six years. It was not unusual for General Custer to ignore her when she was in the room. It was something she had become used to and in truth did not mind. She was devoted to Libbie, but did not like the "Ginnel" as she called him, at all.

"Eliza," she said, "fetch me some more apples. I'm going to need to make more pies."

"Yes'm."

FIVE

When Clint got back to the hotel, the clerk looked at him, curious as to why he had been called into the presence of General Custer. Clint walked up to the desk and leaned on it.

"Looks like I won't miss out on my buffalo hunt after all."

"You're going with the General?" the man asked, surprised.

"That's right, and probably those loud fellas from the East," Clint said. "That is, if one of them is named K. C. Barker."

"Lemme check." The clerk leafed through the registration book. "Yeah, it says right here." He turned the book so Clint could look at it. Sure enough, someone had written "K. C. Barker, Detroit, Michigan."

"The Mayor of Detroit," Clint said.

"Really?" the clerk asked. "How about that?"

Further down the page, Clint also saw the name "P. T. Barnum, New York," and someone had written tomorrow's date as a date of arrival.

"We're waiting for him," he said, pointing to the name.

"Who's he?"

"A very famous man."

"I never heard of him."

"He's famous in the East."

"I ain't never been East."

The clerk pointed to Clint's name.

"I heard of you, though. Who were you supposed to be meeting, anyway?"

"Come on," Clint said. "You didn't read that telegram before you gave it to me?"

The man frowned and said, "No, why would I?"

Clint realized the man was sincere.

"Sorry," Clint said. "It's just that most hotel clerks—hell, most people—would have. I was supposed to be meeting Bat Masterson."

The clerk's eyebrows went up. "I heard of him, too."

"Yeah, well, he can't make it, and now I've been invited to go with Custer, Barker and Barnum, and, I suppose, all those others."

"Mrs. Custer going?"

"Yeah, how did you know?"

"He never leaves her behind if he don't have to," the clerk said. "He's jealous—although I don't know why. It should be the other way around."

"Why's that?"

"Well, she only came out to meet him a little while back. During that time—and this is just a rumor—some say he took a squaw for a mistress. Some say they even had a child."

"Just rumors, right?"

"That's right, but it seems to me *Mrs.* Custer should be the jealous one," the clerk said.

"What's your name?"

"Harry Kelton."

"Harry," Clint said, "maybe we'd be interested in what was going on with Mrs. Custer while General Custer was out here without her."

Harry thought a minute, then said, "You might have a point."

It was getting dark out and it seemed as if someone was shooting off a gun every five minutes.

"How long does that go on?" Clint asked.

"All night."

"*All* night?"

"Well," Harry said, "until pretty late."

"I've got to meet the sheriff who lets that go on all the time," Clint said. "Which way to the sheriff's office?"

"He ain't got an office, really," Harry said. "Just, like, a tent."

"A tent? So there's no jail?"

"Not unless somebody wants to build one. I mean, there's one at the fort, but that's it."

Clint was already too familiar with the "jail" at the fort.

"Okay, then," he said, "which way is his tent?"

Following the clerk's directions he found his way to the tent the sheriff used as an office. Since there was no-where to knock he just stepped inside. A man was sitting at a makeshift desk—a door laid across some boxes—playing solitaire. There was a battered silver star on his shirt.

"Sheriff Latimer?"

The man looked up. He had a full face, with the beginnings of jowls, and little fat pockets under his eyes. He looked to be in his forties.

"What can I do for you?"

"Nothing, I guess," Clint said. "I just wanted to come over and check in with you. Looks like I'm going to be in town for a while."

"And why would that interest me?" He looked down at his game, but seemed to have lost his train of thought.

"Red ten on blackjack," Clint said.

"Oh, thanks."

"My name is Clint Adams."

The lawman had just laid the red ten on the blackjack and he looked up quickly, squinting. The only light in the tent came from a storm lamp on his desk.

"Are you shittin' me?"

"No," Clint said, "I'm not."

"You're the Gunsmith?"

"That's me."

Latimer chuckled and shook his head.

"What brings you to this hell hole?"

"I was going to meet a friend and do some buffalo hunting," Clint said, "but he's not going to show up."

"So then what would keep you here?"

Clint looked around and saw some holes in the sides of the tent that looked like bullet holes. He realized a bullet could come tearing through the canvas at just about any time.

"I got invited to another buffalo hunt."

"By who?"

"General Custer."

"You know the General?"

"Just met him today."

"And you're going hunting with him?"

"And some friends of his."

"Fast company," Latimer said. "I ain't never got invited to no buffalo hunt with the General and his Mrs."

"What makes you think she's going?"

Latimer chuckled again. "He don't go nowhere without her. He's the jealous type—though, I wonder if she knows about his little squaw."

"I thought that was a rumor."

"A rumor everybody's heard," he said.

They paused as the sound of shooting outside stopped.

"Quiet moment," Clint said.

"Ain't many of them."

"Can't you do something about it?"

"Like what?" Latimer asked. "Go out there and get my ass shot off?"

"Don't you have any deputies?"

"Nope," Latimer said, "this shithole of a town ain't got the money for deputies. They barely got the money for me."

"Why'd you take the job?"

Latimer spread his arms and said, "Because this palace came with it. It ain't much, but it's a roof over my head. Without it, I *would* be out there, maybe getting' my head shot off."

"So you never try to stop it?"

"Never," Latimer said, going back to his game, "but you can try, if you like. Maybe they'll listen to you. Of course, you might have to shoot somebody just to get everyone's attention."

"I'll try to avoid that."

"Well, thanks for stoppin' in," Latimer said. "Nice to know we got us a famous man in town."

"Sure," Clint said, "glad to oblige."

He stepped out of the tent and breathed the fresh air. The tent had been warm, and it had been some time since the sheriff had taken a bath.

At least he knew how what kind of law Hays City had—next to none.

SIX

Clint had been in many towns like Hays City, and he was not a man to let the sound of gunshots force him into his room. He left the sheriff's office and went in search of the nearest saloon. At the moment, a cold beer was the only thing on his mind.

The saloon he found had a makeshift sign over the entrance that said SALOON NUMBER 8. In towns like Hays, many saloons didn't bother with names when they could just slap a number on them, just for the purpose of identification. If somebody had a good time at a particular saloon, he should at least be able to tell a friend to meet him at "Saloon Number 8."

When Clint entered, he saw that the place was a hybrid, built half of wood and half of canvas. Perhaps one would begin to devour the other at some point, but at the moment it looked pretty much half and half.

31

It took Clint a few minutes to attract the attention of a bartender and get a beer. When he finally did get the beer he found—to his delight—that it was cold.

He turned with the beer in hand to survey the setup. Lots of gaming tables were going. For a place that was able to afford roulette wheels and game setups, it was a wonder they hadn't purchased a real bar and built a real saloon.

"Attention to detail."

He turned at the sound of the voice. It was deep, husky even, but it was definitely a woman. When he saw her he knew she was *all* woman. She had lots of black hair, worn down so that it tumbled over her creamy white shoulders and even hid some—but not all—of her smooth, white cleavage.

"I beg your pardon?"

"You were wondering why there's canvas and a bar made out of doors, and yet real and—I might add—expensive gaming equipment."

He hesitated a moment and then said, "You sound more like you own the place rather than work here."

"I do own it," she said, with a nod, "but thanks for the compliment. In case you hadn't noticed, the girls here are all young and pretty."

"Your point being?"

She smiled.

"That I'm flattered you thought I worked here."

"I thought you were the star."

"Sorry," she said, "just the proprietor."

"So then you *can* answer my questions."

"Which questions are those?"

"The ones you just told me I was thinking."

"Oh, those questions," she said. "Well, we never

know whether a place is going to be permanent or not, but we do know that men are going to gamble. So when we move to a new place we bring all of our equipment, and we don't spend much money on the roof we put over it—until we're sure that we're going to stay."

"And have you ever?"

"Ever what?'

"Stayed?"

"Not yet," she said.

"Why not?'

"We still haven't found a place where we want to set up for good," she said. "A place to call home."

"And when you say we, you mean you and . . . your partner?"

"Yes."

"And your partner is a man?"

"Right again?"

"And is he just your partner or . . . more?"

"Certainly not more . . ."

"Ah."

"But he is also my husband."

"Oh."

"Does that make a difference?"

"I guess it would . . . to him," he said. "Are you saying it doesn't to you?"

"Are you saying it won't to you if it doesn't to me?"

Clint frowned.

"I think I've forgotten what I'm saying."

"Well, then," she said, "we can just shelve the discussion until another time. Why don't you take a look around, see if you like anything, and the second beer will be on the house."

"And what did I do to deserve that?"

"You came into my place, Mr. Adams."

"Oh," he said, "you know who I am?"

"I've seen you in two other towns where we've had similar setups," she said, "but you never noticed me."

"Really?" He frowned. "I find that hard to believe."

"You've never seemed to have any trouble finding women, that I was able to see," she said. "Beautiful women."

"Well, you certainly qualify."

"Thank you."

"Were you married those times, as well?"

"Unfortunately."

"It doesn't sound like a happy union."

"Let's just say the business part of the partnership is much more successful," she said. "I have to mingle. Stay a while?"

"It should take me that long to look around and have my second beer."

"Good," she said. She put her hand on his arm. "I'll see you later, then."

"I'll be here."

As she turned and walked away, he wondered if her being married was really going to make all that much of a difference to him after all.

SEVEN

Clint got his second beer, looked around, and saw that she was right. The girls there were young and very pretty, but he didn't see one he would have preferred to the proprietor—if she had been available.

The place had everything for the gambler but the one game he was the most interested in—poker. At least, there was no house game. He didn't know if the house allowed private games to start up. They probably wouldn't have liked anything to compete with their blackjack, faro, roulette, and other games that were going on—like Red Dog and Pachinko.

He took a walk around the entire place and by the time he found himself back at the bar he was finished with his free beer and bought another. This time when someone sidled up alongside of him it was a man. He was the woman's age—early thirties—and also had lots of dark hair, only his was cut short.

"I was told you were here," he said, "but wanted to check it out for myself."

"I'm here," Clint said, "but am I who you think I am?"

"The Gunsmith, right?"

"Right."

The man put out his hand.

"I'm Fred Hooper, the owner . . ."

"I met another owner . . ."

"My wife, Kate," Hooper said. "I know. She's the one who told me you were here."

"Why is that such hot news?"

"Well, a man of your reputation coming into our establishment can only do us some good."

"Really?"

"Well . . . unless you killed somebody . . . but then that would probably benefit us, as well." Hooper leaned in and lowered his voice. "You're not going to kill anyone, are you?"

"Not if I can help it." Clint matched the volume level of the man's voice.

"Good, good."

"Your sheriff probably wouldn't like it."

"Latimer?" Hooper asked. "Have you met him?"

"Actually, I have," Clint said.

"Then you know the answer to that."

"I guess I do."

"We tend to take care of things ourselves around here."

"Private security?"

"All around us."

Clint looked around with a different eye. Now he saw that there were men in the saloon who were not paying any attention to the gambling or the girls. They were paying attention to the customers.

"They blend in well," Clint said.

"Thanks," Hooper said. "We don't really want people knowing that they're here. We want them to have a good time, but we want to be ready for anything."

"I don't blame you," Clint said. "Seems like a sound business practice."

"Care for another beer?" Hooper asked. "On the house."

"No, thanks," Clint said. "This is my third. I tend to keep my wits about me as much as possible."

"I can understand that," Hooper said. "Perhaps you'll sit at a table with me, have a cup of coffee and listen to a business proposition?"

Clint didn't really want to listen to a business proposition, but sitting down with a cup of coffee did not sound like a bad idea.

"All right."

"Excellent," Hooper said. "We keep a table in the back open just for us. Kate is already there, waiting."

"You were pretty sure I'd say yes?"

"I was pretty sure you'd listen," Hooper said with a smile, "or that you might just want a cup of coffee."

"Well then, lead the way," Clint said. "We wouldn't want to keep the lady waiting."

EIGHT

As promised, Kate Hooper was sitting at the back table waiting for them, but there was an extra added attraction. There was also a blond woman with her, probably five or six years younger than Kate—in her late twenties. She had long, straight hair and a peaches-and-cream complexion, and her cleavage rivaled that of the older woman.

"Good," Kate said, "you persuaded him to join us."

"It wasn't hard," Hooper said, "apparently he really likes coffee."

The table had a wooden privacy rail around it, so that they had elbow room and breathing space and there was no chance they'd be jostled. Two chairs had been left empty for them, and one of them afforded Clint the opportunity to sit with his back to the wall. Without giving him a choice, Hooper took the other chair.

As they sat, another girl, younger than both Kate and the blonde, came over with a tray bearing a pot of coffee and four cups. She set them out, poured them full, left the pot and went off to do something else.

"Clint," Kate said, "this is my friend, Savannah."

"Very nice to meet you, Mr. Adams," the blonde said. "I've heard a lot about you."

"That gives you the advantage, Savannah," Clint said, "because I've heard nothing at all about you."

"Savannah is a dear friend," Kate said, placing what Clint thought was a proprietary hand on the woman's arm, "who has agreed to come here and work for us. She's a wonderful performer."

"Performer?" Clint asked.

"A singer," Savannah said.

"Will you be singing tonight, then?" Clint asked.

"I'm afraid she won't start until tomorrow," Kate said. "That's when her piano player arrives."

"And my piano," Savannah added.

"Can't do much singing without them, I guess." Clint tried the coffee and found it surprisingly good. He looked around. "Is business this good every night?"

"This is pretty much how it is each night," Hooper said, "but we expect it to get even better once the men in town get a look at—and give a listen to—Savannah."

The blonde, apparently embarrassed, had the good grace to lower her eyes. Clint had the feeling, though, that she was performing even now.

"I didn't have the chance to check out any of the other places in town," Clint said. "How's your competition?"

"There are several other establishments in town," Hooper said, "but only one offers any real competition."

"That should change, though, now that we've brought Savannah in," Kate Hooper said.

"Thanks for not putting pressure on me," Savannah said.

"You know you'll pack them in, dear," Kate said, putting an arm around her friend and giving her a hug.

Being this close to two such beautiful women was starting to have an effect on Clint. He looked at Fred Hooper.

"You said something about a business proposition?"

Hooper looked at his wife, who nodded.

"Should I leave?" Savannah asked.

"Only if business talk will bore you," Hooper said.

"I think I'll leave, then."

They waited while she stood up and bent to kiss each of the Hoopers on their cheeks, giving Clint a very clear view of her impressive cleavage. She then graced him with a big smile.

"I hope to see you again, Mr. Adams."

"When you do," he said, "just call me Clint."

"I'll remember that," she said.

They all watched her walk away and Clint wondered what kind of relationship existed between the three of them.

"All right, then," Hooper said, "to business."

NINE

"We'd like you to come to work for us," Fred Hooper said.

"In what capacity?"

"Head of security."

"Don't you have one?"

"Me, for now," Hooper said. "I've been looking to hire someone because I've got enough to do without overlooking security as well."

"We would pay you very well," Kate added.

"It's not a question of money," Clint said. "I didn't come to Hays City looking for work."

"Why did you come," Hooper asked, "if I may be so bold?"

"I was supposed to meet a friend here to do some buffalo hunting."

"But?" Kate Hooper asked.

"He didn't show up."

"So now you're stuck with nothing to do?" Fred Hooper asked.

"That's actually not the case," Clint said. "I did get an invitation to go buffalo hunting."

"From who?"

"General Custer."

Both of the Hoopers sat back and stared at him.

"You know Custer?" Fred finally asked.

"Just met him today, when he invited me."

"How did he know you were in town?"

"I had to pass a sentry post to get in," Clint said. "Word got back to him."

"Don't take this the wrong way," Hooper said, "but why did he invite you to go hunting with him?"

"Apparently he's got some friends from back East who have come to town to do some hunting," Clint said. "One of them is the mayor of Detroit."

"Michigan," Kate said.

"I know where Detroit is, dear," Hooper said.

She looked away and said, "Sorry," but she said it with a slight smirk.

"Also a man named P. T. Barnum."

"I know that name," Hooper said.

"I do, too."

"We all do," Kate said. "Why is Barnum coming here?"

"Reading between the lines," Clint said, "I think Custer might have invited him to come."

"And now he wants to add you to the part," Hooper said.

"I suppose."

There were a few moments of awkward silence at the

table and then Fred Hooper said, "Well, what about after your hunt? You could come to work for us then."

"I appreciate the offer, but I don't think so."

"Why not?"

"I'm not really looking to settle down in one spot for a long period of time," Clint said.

"Well, that would be perfect," Hooper said, "because we have no idea how long we're gonna be here."

"I realize that," Clint said, "but—"

"Fred, dear," Kate Hooper said, putting her hand on her husband's, "why don't you let me talk with Clint alone for a few minutes. Maybe I can persuade him to change his mind."

Hooper took his hand from beneath his wife's and then patted hers.

"If anyone can, my dear," he said, "I'm sure it's you. Will you excuse me for a moment?" he asked Clint.

"Of course."

He and Kate waited until Fred had stood up and left the table before speaking again.

"Clint."

"Yes."

"If you came to work for us we'd pay you handsomely."

"As I said before, Kate," Clint replied, "it's not the money."

"There would also be . . . other compensations."

Clint sat back.

"Really? Like what?"

"You want me to spell it out?"

"Please do," Clint said. "I'd like to hear the whole offer."

"Well . . . for starters, there's . . . me."

"And?"

"Savannah."

He stared at her.

"And both of us . . . at the same time."

He shifted in his chair. This offer was becoming more and more difficult to refuse.

"And that offer only comes with the job?" he asked. She smiled.

"Well, we're talking about a job right now," she replied, "aren't we?"

They matched stares for a few moments, and then Clint shook his head regretfully.

"Why are you shaking your head?"

"Because I must be crazy," he answered, "but I'm still going to have to turn your offer down."

"Really?" She sounded amazed.

"Really."

"Why?"

"I have this very uncomfortable feeling that I'd be walking in on the middle of something," he said, standing up. "Would you tell your husband I said goodnight?"

TEN

Clint felt somehow relieved to be away from the Hoopers and their friend Savannah. He didn't want to work for them, and he didn't think he wanted them as friends. He would, however, have gladly jumped into bed with either woman, as long as there were no longstanding consequences to be paid later.

Upon leaving the saloon he decided to simply go back to his hotel room and get some sleep. Tomorrow he'd be hearing from Custer about the hunt and, maybe, he'd be meeting P. T. Barnum. He wanted his wits about him when *that* happened.

When Fred Hooper returned to the table he stared at his wife, Kate.

"Where did he go?"

Glumly, chin in hand, elbow on the table, she said, "I think we scared him away."

"That's too bad," Hooper said. "It would have been great if we could have advertised that he was working here."

"Well," she said, "I guess that's not going to happen." She stood up.

"Where are you off to?" he asked.

She smiled.

"I assume Savannah is waiting in our room."

"I still have some work to do," he said, "so I'll have to join the two of you later on."

"That's all right, dear," she said, "I'm sure we can manage."

That's what he was worried about, he thought as he watched her go, the two women would find out they *could* get along without him . . . too well!

When George Armstrong Custer joined his wife in bed that night she cuddled up against him and said, "The day after tomorrow will be very exciting."

"I'm sure it will be," he said, "but we still have tomorrow to get through."

"What possible problems could tomorrow bring?"

"P. T. is not the easiest man to like, Libbie," Custer said. "He and Adams will have to get along or it could ruin the hunt."

"And the other men?" she asked. "That mayor of Detroit and his friends?"

"Barker is friends with Barnum," Custer said. "We'll have to see to it that they have a good time as well."

"When you invited Barnum," she asked, "did you tell him to bring all his friends?"

"There are just a few, Libbie, dear," Custer said, "just a few."

As her husband drifted off to sleep, Libbie Custer thought that his idea of a few and hers were totally different.

As Clint walked down the hall to his room, he could hear the voices of the other men from the other end of the hall. He stared down the hall and saw that several of the room doors were open and a few of the men were standing in them, having a loud discussion. He wondered why other guests in the hotel did not complain.

He opened his door and entered his room and stopped short when he saw Savannah in his bed.

"Good evening," she asked. "Are you in for the night?"

He closed the door and put the hotel key on the dresser.

"Aren't your friends going to miss you?"

"Probably," she said. She was sitting in the bed with the bedsheet held up to her neck. Her odors filled the room—something sweet and something tart. Her skin was luminous in the light from the lamp by the bed. "I suppose they'll just have to make do with each other."

"They *are* married, aren't they?" he asked.

"Oh yes," she said, "they're quite married. They're also quite incompatible and don't get along very well . . . except when it comes to business. When it comes to that they are both quite brilliant together."

"Is that a fact?"

"I have seen them build a business up from nothing," she said.

"You've worked for them before?"

"Many times."

"In other saloons?"

"Saloons, gambling houses, theaters," she said, "whatever business they happened to be in at the time."

"I see."

"Did they manage it?"

"Manage what?"

"To hire you?"

"No."

"Why not?"

"I don't like being used."

She frowned.

"That is what they do, isn't it?"

"You would know that better than I would."

"Yes, they do use people," she said with a nod, "but then, that's why we get along so well. You see, I use them as well."

"In what way?"

She smiled lasciviously and said, "In many ways. Did Kate make her final offer to you?"

"You mean her and you at the same time? Yes, she did."

Savannah looked surprised.

"And you turned that down?" she asked. "You're quite a man, Clint Adams."

"It wasn't easy," he said, "but yes, I turned it down . . . and now look."

"Yes," she said, dropping the sheet away from her, "look. You get one of the prizes after all."

He stood there staring at her. She was breathtaking. Her breasts were firm and large, with heavy round undersides and large, pink nipples. Her skin was so pale it seemed to glow. The scents wafting up from her were

getting stronger, and sharper, and his body was begin-
ning to respond . . . and yet, he hesitated.

"What's the catch?" he asked.

"Catch? There's no catch."

"The Hoopers dangle you in front of me as bait for a
job and a half an hour later you're here ready to give
yourself to me for free?"

"Why is that so hard to believe? You're an attractive
man."

"You have other options."

She made a face.

"Not tonight," she said. "Those options are for later.
Tonight, I want to make my own choice . . . and I choose
you."

She got up on her knees and for a moment he saw
the fair patch of hair between her thighs, where the sharp
scent was coming from—the scent of a woman's read-
iness.

"Is that so hard to believe?" she asked. "Or to take?"

"Hard to believe, maybe," he said, undoing his belt,
"but not hard to take at all."

ELEVEN

When Clint woke the next morning, Savannah was still there. They hadn't talked much after his pants had come off. She had simply proven to him that she was the most uninhibited woman he had ever been in bed with. There were times when he wasn't sure he could match her energy, but in the end he did, again . . . and again . . . and again.

He propped himself up on one elbow and looked down at her. She was lying on her back with her hands up over her head, under the pillow. Her breasts, though large, were incredibly firm and did not sag to the side while she was on her back. He found that as incredible as her energy.

He leaned over and ran his tongue over her left breast, along the underside, around her nipple without touching it and then, finally, right on the nipple itself. He then repeated this on the right breast, but this time when he got to the nipple he suckled it, and then bit it.

"Ow!" she cried. "All right, you caught me. I'm awake!"

"Why are you playing possum?"

"I just wanted to see what you'd do."

He slid his hand down between her legs, rubbing her through the sheet.

"And what do you think of what I'm doing?"

"Mmmm," she said, wriggling her butt, "I approve."

"Maybe you'll approve of this more," he said, and slid his hand under the sheet. He found her wet and ready and slid his middle finger inside of her while stroking her with his thumb. She caught her breath, caught her bottom lip between her teeth and moaned.

He started kissing her breasts again, this time in earnest. He bit them, and it was like biting ripe melons—and even sweeter. With his left hand between her legs he used the right to toss the sheet off of her so he could see her in all her naked glory. She had wonderfully full, rounded thighs and, sometime during the night, he'd had her marvelous ass in his hands, while he lifted her off the bed so he could attack her with his mouth.

Another time he had been on his knees behind her, grasping both hips as she rammed her butt into his belly again and again and again.

Now he slithered down her body to see what she tasted like first thing in the morning. If anything, she was even sweeter. He kept his hand on her and used his mouth at the same time. Eventually she lifted her butt off the bed and reached down to grab his head and grind his face into her crotch while waves of pleasure washed over her.

Still later that morning she returned the favor. Even though they had made love many times during the night, she had no trouble bringing him almost painfully erect with her mouth, sucking him deep inside and then sliding her lips up and down on him with excruciating care. She stroked the area just beneath his testicles with two fingers of her right hand while sucking him, and fondled his balls with her left. When he looked down at her he could see the length of his penis sliding in and out of her mouth, and that was the last straw. That, along with the several different sensations she was treating him to with her hands and her mouth made him sport so powerfully that it literally curled his toes, something he'd heard women admit to having felt, but never before experiencing it himself.

No matter what happened in Hays City from this point on, this made the entire trip worth it.

Or so he thought at the time.

He watched her get dressed, a simple pleasure he'd discovered just recently.

"Are you sure you can't stay?"

"Like I said last night," she told him, "my friends are going to miss me. I'll have to go and explain what happened to me last night."

"And what will you tell them?"

She smiled.

"I'll say I was trying to persuade you to take the job they were offering you. They'll believe that."

"Is that what this was?"

She straightened her skirt and came to him to kiss his mouth softly. At the same time she reached down and stroked his penis with her nails. He couldn't help but react and rise to her touch.

"I don't care if you never work for them," she said, against his mouth. "I only care that I'll be welcome back here tonight."

"Oh," he said, reaching for her, "I think I can assure you of that."

"Good," she said, dancing away from his grasp, "then I'll see you then."

Before he could say another word, she was out the door and gone.

TWELVE

Clint was getting dressed when he heard the stage pull in outside the hotel. That's when he realized how late it really was—almost eleven. He'd never spent that long in bed before. But then, he'd never been in bed with Savannah before. It was a special experience, to say the least.

He walked to the window and looked outside as he pulled on his shirt. He saw a man with wild, graying hair step down from the stage and be greeted by a group of men. After a moment he recognized the men as the noisy easterners who were staying in the rooms down the hall. Was this, then, the famous P. T. Barnum?

Clint waited to see if a woman got off the stage with him, but one did not. He also watched while the stage driver struggled to get a huge trunk down from the top of the coach and into the hands of some of the men who were meeting Barnum—for Clint now assumed that this could be no one else.

Even from here Clint was able to see the flamboyance of the man. He waved his arms theatrically as he spoke, but Clint noticed that the man never once embraced any of the other men. He thought that this told him something about the man. Later, perhaps he'd figure it out.

He went back to the bed, sat on it and pulled on his boots. He hoped he'd be able to get a decent breakfast somewhere at this hour and pushed P. T. Barnum and his friends from his mind. He'd be meeting them soon enough.

As it turned out he was able to get breakfast right in the hotel dining room. Apparently, others rose as late as he had done, and it was not as unusual as he had first thought. Well, it *was* unusual for him, but not at all an unusual occurrence.

After a passable steak and eggs and some very bad coffee he walked through the lobby of the hotel and stepped outside, stopping right there to take a deep breath. Suddenly, there was a flurry of motion as a group of men crossed the street, the wild-haired man among them. They were so deep in conversation that they would have run him down if he had not moved out of the way.

All of the men ignored him except for the wild-haired man he assumed to be P. T. Barnum.

"Your pardon, good sir," Barnum paused to say. "I fear my friends have left their manners back east. Please, accept my pardon."

"I accept, sir," Clint said. "No harm done."

"Excellent," Barnum said. "I see not all Westerners are savages, as I was told back east."

"Some of us can even read, Mr. Barnum," Clint said.

"Ah, you know me?" This obviously pleased the man.

"Just by reputation."

"And which reputation would that be, my good man?"

"Let me see, what did that newspaper call you?" Clint said. "Oh, yes, it was a Denver newspaper and they called you the 'Master of Humbug.' "

"I saw that story," Barnum said. "It was in a New York paper. The Denver paper must have reprinted it."

"No doubt."

"What else have you heard me called here in the West?"

"Do you really want to know?"

"Please," Barnum said, "enlighten me." The man's eyes were very wide, almost childlike, as he waited for Clint to impart the information.

"Well . . . let me think . . . Charlatan . . . I've heard that one . . . Liar . . . ah, Deceiver, I heard that one, too . . . oh yes, Cheat . . ."

"What?" Barnum asked. "Nothing good?"

"Showman," Clint said. "I heard that one. Is that a good one?"

Barnum smiled and said, "My good sir, that is the best!"

Obviously happy with that word and ignoring the rest, Barnum went into the hotel to catch up with his friends, leaving Clint to ponder his first meeting with the man he would be buffalo hunting with the next day.

Barnum had exuded a youthful energy, even though— from appearances—he must have been sixty. Clint wondered what the ultimate showman was doing in Kansas for a buffalo hunt. Or was there some other reason he was there?

Clint decided to take a walk through the town and eventually ended up at the livery stable to check on his horse. The animal had seemed winded when they rode into town, and if he was going to use him on the hunt he wanted to make sure the animal was in good shape.

He stepped down from the boardwalk in front of the hotel, picked a direction and started walking.

Later, he was on his way to the stable when he saw a woman walking toward him. He was surprised to see the way men stepped out of her way and treated her respectfully, even two men who were arguing who stopped the argument long enough to tip their hats as she went by and then went back to their argument.

Kate Hooper was obviously well thought of by the men in Hays City.

She smiled as they approached each other. She was wearing a high-necked dress that clung to her waist, accentuating her full bosom. Her long dark hair was worn down and flowed past her shoulders. At the very least she appeared to be a dark-haired version of Savannah. He was surprised the women were close friends—despite whatever *other* aspects there were to their relationship.

"You're a very bad man," she said, as they stopped to talk.

"And why is that?"

"You kept Savannah out all night long."

"Why does that make me bad and not her?"

"She's very impressionable," Kate said. "You obviously seduced her."

"Is that what she said?"

"Of course not," Kate answered. "She said it was her

idea, but I knew what kind of man you were as soon as I saw you."

"Is that a fact?" he asked. "Are you ever wrong when you make judgments like that?"

"No," she said, "never."

"Never?"

She shook her head.

"Not when it comes to men."

"I see."

"I don't suppose she was able to change your mind about taking that job?" she asked, hopefully.

"I'm afraid not," Clint said, "although she did try her very best."

"I'm sure she did," Kate said. "She looked very . . . tired when I saw her, but also very . . . satisfied."

"My specialty," he said, with a touch of maliciousness, "satisfying women."

Kate Hooper made a sound in her throat that he felt right down to his groin and gave him a hot look with her dark, smoldering eyes.

"Lucky girl," she said.

"I don't expect you have any problem in that area, Kate." If she was bold enough to want to discuss sex out in the open, he decided to see if she would be that bold with her own sex life.

"Oh, you'd be surprised," she said, smiling. "It takes a lot to satisfy me."

"I suppose your husband works hard at it."

"He works hard at a lot of things, but unfortunately I'm not one of them," she said wistfully. "But I'll give him a break—I don't think he has the capability to satisfy me even if he wanted to."

"Then why stay married to him?"

"Because marriage is about a lot more than just sex," she said. "When it comes to that, I usually have to look . . . elsewhere."

That line was accompanied by another hot, hungry look.

"I'm sure there are men lining up to see if they're up to the task."

"There is no shortage of men, that's true," she said, "but most of them wouldn't know the first thing about satisfying a woman."

Clint wondered just how much Savannah had told her friend Kate about their night together.

"Where are you going now?" she asked. He wondered if she was actually going to ask him to give it a try.

"To the livery to check on my horse," Clint said. "I want to see if I'll be needing a fresh mount for tomorrow."

"Fresh mount . . ." she repeated, making it sound suggestive. "Do you mind if I walk with you?"

"To the livery?"

"I have a horse there," she said. "A filly named Dora. I like to check on her from time to time. May I?"

"Be my guest."

"May I take your arm?"

He extended his arm and she slid hers though it. They walked through town to the livery that way.

THIRTEEN

When they were approaching the livery, Clint asked, "You don't worry about walking around a town like this alone?"

She laughed and said, "No. Any man who treated me with anything less than respect would not be allowed into my place. Besides, I never do it at night. Even the most respectful men become something else at night, and after a few drinks."

When they reached the livery a man stepped out to greet them. He was the same man Clint had turned his gray over to.

"Afternoon, Miz Kate."

"Hello, James."

"Come to have a look at Dora?"

"Yes, and Mr. Adams would like to see his horse."

"Sure thing. You know where Dora is, and this fella's

gray is about two stalls away. That's one worn-out horse, Mister."

"I was afraid of that. Do you have any horses for sale?"

"I got a few. I can't show 'em to you right now, though. I got some errands to run."

"James knows horses, Clint," Kate said. "You could do worse than having him pick one out for you."

Clint looked at the man.

"James—"

"The name's Jimmy," the older man said. "Miz Kate is the only one who calls me James."

"Okay, Jimmy," Clint said, "I need a horse for to-morrow. I'm going on a buffalo hunt with General Cus-ter."

"Do tell?" Jimmy looked unimpressed.

"Can you pick me out a horse to use for the day?" Clint asked. "I'll rent it for the day and if I like it I'll probably buy it."

"You can do that, can't you, James?" Kate Hooper put her hand on the man's arm, and Clint saw him just melt beneath her gaze.

"Yes, Ma'am," he said, "if you say so."

"There," Kate said, "now you don't have to check on your horse."

"You wanted to see yours, though."

"I trust James," she said. "How is Dora doing, James?"

"Jest fine, Ma'am."

"There, you see?" She took Clint's arm. "Thank you, James."

"Sure thing, Miz Kate."

"Come on, Clint," she said, tugging at his arm.

As they moved away from the livery, Clint said, "Where are we going?"

"To your hotel room."

"Kate—"

"Oh shut up about me being married," Kate said. "Savannah told me some of the things you did to her last night, and I'm all wet just thinking about it. We're going to your room and you are going to pin my ankles behind my ears if I have to kill you to get you to do it."

How could Clint refuse an offer like that?

FOURTEEN

It may have just been a figure of speech for Kate, but she did end up with her ankles pinned back almost to her ears.

When they got into his room she was all over him, using one hand to tear at his clothes and the other to tear at her own, all the while saying, "Hurry, hurry, Jesus, hurry."

She had been telling him the truth on the street. When they were naked and he slid his hand down between her legs he found her soaking wet. Under other circumstances, with another woman, he might have just threw her down on the bed and rammed himself into her, but he already knew that Kate Hooper was a rare woman. She knew what she wanted when it came to sex and wasn't afraid to talk about it. He had not run into many women like that, and yet here in Hays City, in two days, he had encountered two.

So instead of dumping her on the bed—which still smelled of Savannah—Clint went down to his knees and pressed his face to her fragrant, wet crotch. He held her hips and poked his nose against her, then stuck out his tongue to taste her. Amazingly, she lifted one left and draped it over his shoulder, opening herself to him and maintaining her balance. His tongue fluttered up and down the length of her moist slit, entered her, then stroked her slowly, poking expertly where it would do the most good. It had only been during the past few years that Clint had discovered this particular way of satisfying a woman. It had been demonstrated to him by an older woman, who had instructed him in the proper technique, and since then he had satisfied many women with it—sometimes to their utter amazement and pleasure.

Kate Hooper was more experienced than most women he'd been with, for she knew enough to open herself to his tongue. When he introduced his finger into the equation, though, it suddenly felt as if her knees—or knee—would give.

He wrapped his arms around her, gripped her butt and lifted her off her feet, even though she was a full-bodied woman and not light by any means. He turned and moved to the bed, depositing her on it, on her back. Once there she spread her legs again, and he knelt beneath them and went to work on her. Before long he had her writhing around, gripping his head with one hand, balling the sheet up in her other, digging her heels into the mattress until finally she let out a long, gutteral scream which had to have been heard all through the hotel.

Good, he thought, *maybe that will disturb some of those noisy Easterners . . .*

Later was when he lifted her legs, pushed her ankles up near her ears and entered her. She was still very wet, and he pierced her easily, sliding into her steaming hot depths. In this position she was about as open to a man as a woman could get, and at one point she even took her ankles in her hands to spread herself wider.

"Harder, oh harder," she said then, gripping her own ankles tightly, "harder, faster, come on!"

He obliged, driving himself into her harder and faster until finally he exploded inside her, lunging at her, emptying himself into her, and still she wouldn't let him withdraw. She released her ankles so she could wrap her legs around him, and her arms, and she held him there, breathing heavily into his ear, their flesh damp and stuck together.

Then it was her turn to give him pleasure, and she went at her task with abandon. She used her tongue on him everywhere, even places he'd never felt a woman's tongue before. In no time he was hard again, harder than before, and she took him into her mouth and began to suck him avidly. He looked down, saw himself gliding in and out of her mouth, thought briefly of a similar scene the night before with Savannah and at that point could not have said which woman had given him more pleasure. All he knew was that he was glad he had gone to bed with each of them, and now the offer that had been made to him if he took the job at the saloon came to mind, and he thought that his chances were very good of seeing it happen without having to take the job.

Sometimes, life is *very* fair.

"Oh my God," Kate said sometime later.

"Yeah," Clint said.

"Savannah was so right," she said, "and yet she wasn't right enough."

"So you talked about it, huh?"

"Sweetie, women talk about everything to each other," she said, "especially their men."

"So what did she tell you?"

"Just like a man," she said. "You want to hear what we say about you."

He waited.

"She said that you were something very rare and very special," she went on, "a man who cared about a woman's pleasure as much—maybe even more—than your own."

"And that's good, huh?"

"Oh, baby," she said, rolling toward him so that his arm was caught between her ample breasts, "that is *very* good."

Her breasts looked and felt so good—as large and as firm as Savannah's but with dark brown nipples—that he realized he had not spent enough time on them. He rolled over, took them in his hands and lowered his mouth to them, and spent the next half hour making up for that.

FIFTEEN

Kate said she had to get to the saloon to set up for the day's business. She dressed while he watched and left him feeling spent on the bed, which now smelled of two women, Savannah and Kate, each one very distinctive.

Clint could not believe his luck, running into two women like *these* two in the same place and on the same day. It certainly made the trip to town even more worth it than that morning when he had watched Savannah dress and leave. Of course, he had just bedded down another man's wife, but somehow he didn't think he was going to be faced with an irate husband at any time during his stay in Hays City.

He rolled over in the bed, from Kate's scent to Savannah's scent, and found himself getting hard still again. Almost embarrassed because he was aroused and all alone in his room, he quickly left the bed and got

71

himself dressed. Even though he was a young man, the hours he had spent with the two women since last night had taken its toll on him.

He was hungry.

As he left the hotel he saw Corporal John Hailey walking toward the hotel. At first he thought there was little doubt as to who he was coming to see, but then he realized it could be either him or Barnum. He stayed where he was until Hailey mounted the boardwalk and saw him.

"Good afternoon, Corporal," he said.

"Mr. Adams," Hailey said. "Just the man I was coming to see."

"I thought you might have been coming to see P. T. Barnum."

"Oh, no," Hailey said. "The general and Mr. Barnum have already spoken. They're all set for tomorrow. I'm here to deliver a message to you from the general."

"And what's that?"

"He would like you to be in the fort at eight A.M. tomorrow morning to meet with everyone for the hunt."

"He's getting all those Easterners up that early?"

"Yes, sir."

"Well, you tell the general I'll be there."

"Yes, sir."

"Tell me something, Corporal."

"Sir?"

"Will you be going as well?"

"No, sir," Hailey said. "The general doesn't see any reason for me to go."

"How do you feel about that?"

The young man shrugged.

"It's his party, sir," he said. "Besides, I'm not much for hunting. Sir, the general wanted me to ask you if you needed a horse? He said the Army would be happy to supply you with one."

"I've got that taken care of, Corporal," Clint said, "but thank General Custer for me."

"Actually, you could thank him yourself, sir, if you accept his invitation to dinner."

"Dinner? Tonight?"

"Yes, sir," Hailey said. "The invitation comes from both the general and Mrs. Custer. The general thought it would give you a chance to meet the others in the party ahead of time."

"That wouldn't be a bad idea," Clint said. "Tell the general I'd be glad to come to dinner."

"Yes, sir," Hailey said. "I'll let him know. He asks that you come to his quarters at seven."

"Where are his quarters?"

"Right behind his office," Hailey said. "Just go around the building to the back and knock on the door."

"Thanks, Corporal. I'll be there."

"Yes, sir."

"If you get a chance, tell Mrs. Custer 'thank you' for me."

"I'll do that, sir."

Hailey turned and started away, and Clint thought he'd never met a more respectful man or been called "sir" so often in his life.

SIXTEEN

Clint decided that he didn't want to leave the hotel to go and have dinner with the general and his wife because Barnum and his friends would probably be leaving at the same time. Instead, he went over to the livery first to let Jimmy know when he'd be needing the horses they'd agreed he would rent. When he told the older man he needed it at seven thirty in the morning, he just squinted and asked, "That late?"

Jimmy—or "James"—struck Clint as the kind of man who might only like one person in his life, and that person was Kate Hooper.

Once that errand was done he took his time walking over to the fort, hoping that the other guests had arrived before him. It occurred to him that he didn't know how many guests there were. Would the entire crew of men be there, or just Barnum, and perhaps the politician, Barker, the mayor of Detroit? As he approached the general's quarters he realized there was no point in pondering it any further. He was just a matter of minutes from finding out.

He found his way to the entrance to the quarters and knocked on the door. It was opened by a black servant girl.

"Yessuh?"

"My name is Clint Adams," he said. "I'm here for dinner."

"Yessuh. Please come in."

He entered, and she closed the door and turned to face him. She was a cute thing, small but curvy, with a very pretty face.

"What's your name?"

"Eliza, suh." She said it with a curtsy. "I'll take you into the dining room now. The other guests have done already arrived."

"Thank you, Eliza."

He followed her into a small dining room, which was actually the living room, he guessed, since the general's living quarters were not properly set up for entertaining dinner guests. Furniture had been moved to make room for a long wooden table and an appropriate number of chairs.

Already in the room were Custer, Barnum and one of the men Clint recognized from the hotel. Also there was a lovely woman Clint took to be Custer's wife, Libbie.

"Ah, splendid, you've arrived," Custer said, approaching Clint with his hand outstretched. "Let's introduce you to everyone."

He tugged Clint along by the hand until he was facing Mrs. Custer.

"This vision of loveliness is my wife, Libbie."

"Mrs. Custer, it is my pleasure."

"Thank you for accepting our invitation, Mr. Adams, both to dinner and to the hunt."

"I'm honored to have received both."

They moved to the next person.

"This gentleman is K. C. Barker, the mayor of Detroit, Michigan."

"You're a long way from home, sir."

Barker, a florid-faced, thickly built man pumped Clint's hand enthusiastically.

"It's an honor to meet you, sir," Barker said. "Even in Detroit we've heard of the Gunsmith."

"I didn't know my notoriety had spread quite that far" was all Clint could think to say.

"And this is Phineas T. Barnum," Custer said, as they fronted Barnum.

"We've met," Barnum said as they shook hands.

"I didn't know that," Custer said. "When?"

"Just this afternoon, in front of the hotel," Barnum said, releasing Clint's hand. "Mr. Adams was telling me some of the names he has heard me called."

"Well, those couldn't have all been good," K. C. Barker said, with a loud laugh.

"Some good, some bad," Clint said.

"A showman," Barnum said, "that is the one I remember. Actually, I think that was the only good one in the bunch."

Clint looked at the table and saw that there was a chair unaccounted for.

"Is there to be another guest?"

"My second in command, Major North, will be joining us, as soon as he finishes his duties," Custer said.

"He'll also be accompanying us on the hunt."

Clint was impressed. Both the C.O. and his next in line would be going on the hunt with Barnum—and he was sure that this whole buffalo hunt was being put on for the "Showman."

"My dear," Custer said to his wife, "I think we can begin now with drinks."

SEVENTEEN

The general and his wife handed out snifters of brandy to their guests—actually, Eliza did the handing out—and then they sat at the table, except for Libbie Custer, who went into the kitchen with Eliza.

"Libbie insisted on preparing the entire meal herself," Custer said. "She's the world's finest hostess."

"That would serve you well in Washington, General," K. C. Barker said, and then added, "that is, if you have any political aspirations. It's very important for a man to have a fine hostess if he wants to get anywhere in Washington."

"No K. C.," Barnum chimed in, "would you have us believe that it's more important for a man to have a hostess then to have a solid political platform?"

"Once you're in Washington, P. T.," Barker said,

"your political career can survive a change of platform, but not a change of hostess."

"I am appalled," Barnum said. "What about you, General?"

"Well," Custer said, "I suppose I'd have an opinion if I did have political aspirations, but right now my aspirations are limited to Indian fighting."

"And what about you, Mr. Adams?" Barnum asked. "Do you have an opinion on the subject?"

"I'm afraid I have to go along with the general on this one, Mr. Barnum," Clint said.

"Are you an also Indian fighter, then?" Barnum asked.

"No," Clint said, "I was referring to the fact that I have no political aspirations."

"Ah . . ."

At that point there was a knock on the door. Eliza came rushing from the kitchen to answer it and then showed in a soldier who was wearing a major's bars.

"Ah, Major North," Custer said, standing. The two men saluted each other rather than shook hands. "You've competed all your duties for the day?"

"I have, sir." The major looked to be a few years older than Custer, dark-haired, with a mustache not so carefully trimmed as Custer's.

"Then at ease and have a seat, Major. Gentlemen, my second, Major North. From left to right, Major, K. C. Barker of Detroit, P. T. Barnum, late of New York, and Clint Adams."

The major had obviously not heard of either Barker or Barnum, but he had heard of Clint. He nodded to the other two men, but made a point of shaking Clint's hand.

"A pleasure, sir."

"Major."

The man sat down across from Clint, where he would be sitting next to Libbie Custer. Custer got his second some brandy and then resumed his position at the table's head.

"We were discussing politics when you came in, Major," Barnum said, seeming intent on directing the flow of the conversation.

"Why would a showman such as yourself want to discuss politics, Mr. Barnum?" Clint asked. "I'm sure there are countless other subjects we could discuss with you—for instance, your discovery of Tom Thumb."

"Tom Thumb?" Major North asked.

"A fifteen-pound man," K. C. Barker said. "A wonder to behold whom P. T. took to Europe to entertain the crown heads there."

"Gentlemen, gentlemen," Barnum said, raising his hands in a placating gesture, "I am retired from show business and would much rather discuss other matters of the day."

They were saved from discussing anything when Libbie and Eliza walked into the room bearing trays of steaming food. They set the trays on the table where the men could reach them, and then Libbie took her place and they began to eat. Eliza returned to the kitchen and came back with glasses of water for all of them.

From that point on it was Libbie Custer who took control of the conversation, proving that she was—as Custer had pointed out—the perfect hostess.

When Libbie wanted to hear about some of P. T. Barnum's adventures, he had no choice but to speak of them; when she wanted to hear about Clint's travels and adventures, he could not refuse, either. By the time they had coffee, Custer, North and Barker—and Eliza, from aside—had been enthralled by both men's experiences.

Well, perhaps General Custer was not enthralled, but he had listened intently and respectfully as each man spoke.

"If you gentlemen will excuse me," Libbie said, rising, "I will help Eliza bring in the coffee and homemade pie."

"Homemade pie?" Barnum asked. "Splendid. What kind, if I may ask?"

"I've made peach," Libbie said, "and apple."

"Apple is my favorite," Barnum said.

"And peach mine."

Custer did not speak, because his favorite was rhubarb.

"I believe you're right about Mrs. Custer, General," K. C. Barker said, when she had left the room, "she is the perfect hostess."

Custer looked pleased.

Libbie and Eliza returned with coffee and pie and while Clint had tasted better coffee, the peach pie was excellent.

"May I ask some questions about tomorrow, General?" Clint inquired.

"Ask away."

"How many men will be on the hunt?"

"Well," Custer said, "there will be fifty troops with us to make sure we are not interrupted. Other than that there will be we five and—correct me if I am wrong, K. C.—eight other men."

"That's correct," Barker said.

"So thirteen of us actually hunting?"

"Yes."

"And Mrs. Custer will be along?"

"She will remain in camp," Custer said. "We will have a tent erected for her privacy, which I will—of course—share with her. The rest of you will be sleeping beneath the stars."

"Sounds good to me," Barker said.

Clint wondered how long it would be before the mayor of Detroit and his friends complained about sleeping on the hard ground.

After coffee and pie, Custer invited the men into his office for cigars and more drinks.

"Yes, please join him," Libbie pleaded with them. "Eliza and I have a lot of cleaning up to do."

"And will you be joining us afterwards?" P. T. Barnum asked.

"I will join you for a drink," she said, "but alas, I will not be partaking of a cigar—if no one minds."

"Dear lady," Barnum said, "I am sure I speak for all when I say that whatever you wish to do is fine with us."

"Gentlemen?" Custer said. "Will you follow me, please?"

EIGHTEEN

Clint assumed they were gathering in the general's office because the living quarters were too small. The office wasn't that large, either, and with five men in it, it became sort of cramped. There were only three chairs and Custer took the one behind his desk, apologizing for the lack of amenities. Major North chose to remain standing, as did Clint.

"Mr. Barnum and Mr. Barker are our guests here in the West," Clint reasoned, and the two men accepted that reasoning and sat.

"I do insist on one thing, though," Barnum said.

"What's that?" Clint asked.

"That you call me P. T.," Barnum said. "Everyone does."

"And I'm K. C.," Barker chimed in.

Somehow, to Clint, "K. C." sounded dumb for a

grown man to be called, but he didn't feel the same about "P. T." Strange.

Once the men were in their places, the general handed out cigars and, instead of brandy, some good scotch whiskey in shot glasses. It was too good to knock back, though, and they all sipped it.

Barnum became interested in the map of the area that was on the wall.

"Will we be running into any Indians tomorrow, George?" he asked.

Clint wondered how many men there were who could get away with calling Custer by his first name.

"There's always that possibility, Phineas," Custer said. Clint wondered if Custer chose to use Barnum's first name because of the man's comment that "everybody" called him P. T. After all, Custer wasn't "everybody."

"Begging the general's pardon," North said, "if I may speak to that?"

"Go ahead, Major."

North addressed himself to Barnum.

"Sir, we'll be enough of a force to keep any curious Cheyenne, Sioux or Arapaho away from us, I can guarantee that."

"But I don't want them to stay away," Barnum said. "I'd like to see some Indians. Wouldn't you, K. C.?"

"I'm not as curious as you are, P. T.," Barker said. "I'll be satisfied to just do some buffalo hunting."

Barnum studied the map.

"Where is the area we'll be hunting in?"

North went over and pointed the area out to Barnum, and then—upon the showman's request—the areas most likely inhabited by the three tribes.

"Tell me, Phineas," Custer said, drawing the man's attentions away from the map, "how long is *this* retirement going to last?"

"I don't know what you mean, George," Barnum said. "I am retired for good from show business. I have promised this to my loving wife."

"You've made that promise before, P. T." Barker said, "and each time something has lured you from retirement."

"Well, not this time," Barnum assured the man. "I am retired for well and good. You can depend on it."

"I'll believe it when I see it," Barker said.

At that moment the connecting door between the office and the living quarters opened and Libbie Custer came in.

"I hope I'm not interrupting anything, gentlemen."

"Not at all, Madam," Barnum said. "We are enriched by your presence."

"Let me pour you a drink, my dear."

"No, please," she bade her husband. "I simply came to bid you all goodnight. If I don't get enough sleep tonight I will simply be no good to anyone tomorrow when we camp."

"Well then, goodnight," Custer said. He rose from his chair to peck his wife's cheek.

She said goodnight to each of the other men and Clint noticed something. Barnum bent to kiss Libbie's hand, and Clint saw her exchanging a glance with Major North over Barnum's head. Or was it his imagination? He remembered what others had said about Custer's jealousy. Was Custer noticing the same thing? He didn't seem to be. Maybe Clint *was* imagining it.

"Goodnight, gentlemen," she said, for the final time.

At the open door she looked at her husband and asked, "May I send Eliza to bed as well, dear?"

"Very well," Custer said. "I can show the gentlemen out when they leave."

Libbie nodded and went back into the living quarters, closing the door behind her.

"Well," Barker said, "I have pretty much the same problem as Mrs. Custer. I need to get enough sleep."

"I think we all do," Barnum said.

"I can have the major walk you gentlemen back to your hotel," Custer said.

Clint could see that the major did not like that idea at all.

"There's no need for that, General," Clint said. "I'm going back to the hotel as well. We can all walk together."

"Very well," Custer said. He stood. "Let me show you gentlemen out, then, and I will see you all in the morning."

They all walked through the living quarters to the door and left, including Major North, who bade them all goodnight outside.

They walked back through the fort to Hays City, and then along the main street to the hotel. At the door Barker started in, but Barnum stopped.

"P. T.?"

"You go ahead, Barker," Barnum said. "I'm not quite ready to turn in, yet."

"Well, all right. Goodnight, then."

"Do you know of a good saloon in town?" Barnum asked Clint.

"As it happens, I do," Clint said.

"I'll buy you a drink, then, unless you're ready to turn in?"

"No, not quite yet."

"Well then, lead on, Mr. Adams, lead on."

NINETEEN

Clint took Barnum over to Saloon Number 8, Kate and Fred Hooper's place. Being underneath a tarp—even partially—was nothing new for P. T. Barnum.

"Drink or gamble?" Clint asked.

"Drink," Barnum said. "Gambling has never been a lure for me—not *games* of chance, anyway."

"Just your life?"

"Is there a bigger gamble?"

"Not that I know of."

They went to the bar, made some room for the two of them and ordered a couple of beers.

"Why do I get the feeling you want to talk to me about something without anyone else around?" Clint asked.

"Because you're a perceptive man," Barnum said.

"What's the pitch, P. T.?"

91

"I could make a lot of money for you and me," Barnum said.

"How?"

"By putting you on display."

"On display?"

"Your talents," Barnum said, "I meant displaying your talents."

"And which talents are those?"

"The ones you're best known for," Barnum said. "Shooting—and also talking."

"Talking?"

"I was very interested to hear some of the stories you told Libbie Custer tonight," Barnum said. "I believe I can get people to pay to hear you tell those stories, and then to do some shooting."

"What if the stories I told weren't true?" Clint asked.

Barnum smiled and said, "So much the better. I really don't care whether they're true or not, just that people will pay to hear them."

"Then why not just hire someone to pretend to be me and tell the stories?" Clint asked. "If what I've read is true, you don't mind having people pretend to be someone they're not."

He was referring to an early Barnum flimflam when, many years ago, he displayed a black woman who purported to not only be over a hundred years old, but also to have been the nursemaid to a young George Washington.

"The incident you refer to came early in my career," Barnum said, "and I was just as taken in by the woman as everyone else."

When the woman suddenly died, an autopsy had revealed her to be in her sixties or seventies, but certainly nowhere near a hundred.

"Telling stories and target shooting is not the way I want to spend my life, P. T.," Clint said.

"Who said anything about spending your life doing it?" Barnum asked. "I'm talking about a matter of months, perhaps a year. By then you would have all the money you'll ever need."

"I don't know how much that is, P. T.," Clint said. "You've been rich and poor. You tell me how much is all the money a man will ever need?"

Barnum smiled and said, "I don't know. I've never had all I need—not yet, anyway."

"Besides," Clint said, "I thought I heard you saying tonight that you are well and truly retired."

"I would come out of retirement for this," Barnum said. "Clint, I could take you to Europe and make you bigger than Tom Thumb—so to speak."

"I'm sorry, P. T.—"

"Don't turn me down yet," Barnum said, putting his hand on Clint's arm. "Think about it. Tell me after the hunt."

"There's really nothing to think about," Clint said. "I'm a little young to start telling my life story on a stage."

"Not your life story," Barnum said, "just some stories."

"I'm afraid not."

Barnum just stared at Clint, who suddenly became aware of something. Phineas T. Barnum was desperate for *something* to bring him out of retirement.

"P. T.," he said, "if you want to come out of retirement, just do it. You don't need me for that."

"You don't understand," Barnum said. "Barker was right. I have retired and unretired before, and each time it breaks my wife's heart a little more. I need something *big* this time, something even she will be excited about."

"And you think that's me?"

"I *know* it is."

"I wish I could help you, P. T.," Clint said, "I really do."

"All right, look," Barnum said. "I'm not going to bring this up again until after the hunt. Then I'll ask you only one more time. Is that fair?"

"Fair enough, I guess."

Barnum finished his beer and put the empty mug on the bar.

"And now it's time for me to turn in," he said. "I'm not as young as I used to be. I can find my way back to the hotel, though, so you stay."

"All right," Clint said. "I'll say goodnight, then."

Barnum stared at him, opened his mouth to say something, then remembered the promise he had just made.

"Goodnight," he said, and left the saloon.

Clint considered Barnum's offer for about a minute, then shook his head. There was no just way he'd travel the country—or the world—as one of P. T. Barnum's oddities.

There was no way he would do it.

TWENTY

He was having another beer when he spotted Fred Hooper at the same time the man saw him. There was no getting away from him, so he just stood his ground as the man approached.

"Nice to see you back," Hooper said. "Give any thought to my offer?"

"I've been getting a few offers lately," Clint replied, "giving them all some thought."

"Oh? Other job offers?" Clint figured the man knew he'd been to bed with Savannah, but did he know about Kate?

"One other one."

"Taking that one?"

"Turning it down."

"For what reason?"

"Same reason I turned you down," Clint said. "I'm not looking for a job."

"I suppose that's a good reason," Hooper said. "Is there any way I could sweeten the pot?"

"Mr. Hooper," Clint said, "I don't mean any disrespect here, but I really don't see any way I would agree to work here. It's got nothing to do with you, or with your place, or the town—well, maybe the town."

"What's wrong with Hays City?"

"Nothing much, except it's like dozens of other towns I've seen spring up around the West," Clint said. "Some last, some don't, but I'm not the kind of man who will invest very much time in any of them in order to find out. I'm not a speculator in that respect, as you obviously are."

"Indeed, that is what I am," Hooper said, "and I believe Hays City will become something."

"How does Kate feel?"

"She's not so sure," Hooper said, "but she's also a speculator, so she's willing to give it some time. I'm sorry you're not, but I understand that this is not your kind of life. No offense taken."

The man offered his hand, and Clint took it.

"Another beer on the house?" Hooper asked.

Clint put his empty mug down on the bar and said, "No thanks. I've got to turn in. I've got a buffalo hunt early tomorrow morning."

"Well, good luck," Hooper said. "Hunting buffalo has never been something that interested me, but have a good time."

"Goodnight, Mr. Hooper."

"Fred," Hooper said, "please."

"Goodnight, Fred."

Clint left, feeling like a shit for having slept with the man's wife—now that they were on a first-name basis.

TWENTY-ONE

Clint expected to find one of the women in his room—or both. Could it be that both women were still trying to lure him into a job? They'd tried separately, and would they now try together?

He had a bet with himself, and when he opened his door and saw who was in his bed, he won.

"We flipped a coin," Savannah said, "and I won."

"No," he said, undressing, "I think I won."

Although, he figured he would have won either way.

Later in the night he told her about feeling bad that he'd slept with Kate, since she was married to Hooper.

"Tonight he told me to call him Fred," he finished. "That really made me feel bad."

"Well, don't," she said, moving her hand around his belly in a circular motion. "He knows that she does it,

99

and he doesn't care. Their relationship has become purely business . . . most of the time."

"I just won't spend any . . . private time with her anymore, that's all," he said. "It'd be safer all around."

"You'll hurt her feelings."

"Better her feelings get hurt than *somebody* gets hurt," Clint said. "Besides, tomorrow I'm leaving on a buffalo hunt, and I don't know how long I'll be out. Whenever I get back, though, I'll be leaving town."

"So this is our last night together?"

"Looks that way."

She slid her leg over him and mounted him, feeling his penis begin to grow beneath her.

"Then why are we wasting it talking?"

Clint woke in the morning with Savannah breathing softly next to him, lying on her back. She told him that a woman with breasts her size was not comfortable lying on her stomach. That was okay with him because she had kicked the sheet off during the night and looked glorious, lying there on her back with her legs spread. The patch of hair between her legs was an even paler shade of blond than the hair on her head.

He didn't wake her because he wanted to get an early start and knew he wouldn't if she was awake. He dressed quickly and quietly and slipped from the room. Maybe, when he got back from the hunt, he'd make time for just one more night with her.

When he got to the livery, Jimmy had a horse ready, complete with Clint's saddle. Clint had his rifle and saddlebags with him. The horse was a good-sized colt who looked to have some wind in him.

"What is he, five or six?" Clint asked.

"Five. He'll go all day for ya."

"That's probably what I'll need," Clint said.

"His name is—"

"Don't tell me his name," Clint said, holding up his hand. "I don't want to get that personal with a horse."

He fixed his saddlebags and rifle to the saddle and then mounted up. The animal felt good between his legs.

"Settle up now?" he asked.

"When you get back 's soon enough," Jimmy said. "Just remember, you break 'im, you buy 'im."

Clint smiled.

"I'll remember."

He wheeled the colt around and pointed him toward the fort.

TWENTY-TWO

As Clint rode back past the hotel, he sat P. T. Barnum, K. C. Barker and the rest of their party mounting horses that had been brought over to them from the fort. Clint waved as he rode up to them. Barnum had just swung into the saddle and seemed to be sitting on his Army mount comfortably.

"Good morning," Barnum shouted.

" 'Morning, P. T.," Clint said. "Mayor Barker."

Barker seemed to enjoy the respect of his title, so he simply nodded and smiled in greeting.

"Ready for the hunt?" Barnum asked.

"Quite ready."

"I assume you've been buffalo hunting before."

"Many times, yes."

"Good," Barnum said, "I shall count on you for guidance, if you don't mind."

"I don't mind, but Custer might."

"Nonsense," Barnum said, "George will have enough to do without worrying about me."

There were two soldiers and a man who looked like a scout or a buffalo hunter with the party who had brought the horses over. One of the soldiers was Corporal Hailey.

"Good morning, Corporal," Clint greeted, as the man road up to him and Barnum.

"Good morning, sir," he said, then turned his attention to Barnum. "Sir, we should be moving along."

"Lead the way, Corporal, lead the way."

When they reached the fort, Clint saw the rest of the party assembled on the parade ground. Fifty men were in double rank, and sitting on a horse in front of them was Major North. Custer was nowhere in sight, but there was a buggy in front of his headquarters, no doubt for Libbie Custer. Behind the buggy was a supply wagon.

As they rode up to the assemblage, the door to the C.O.'s office opened and Custer stepped out, pulling on a pair of calfskin gloves. His blond hair had been freshly washed and almost gleamed in the sunlight. He turned, put his hand out, and drew Mrs. Custer out the door. She was wearing a full dress, cinched tight at the waist, which showed her off to be very slender. That dress on either Savannah or Kate would have started a riot on the grounds.

"Gentlemen," Custer greeted, after helping Libbie up onto the buggy, "welcome. I assume you're all ready for the hunt?"

Clint, who had done some reading in his spare time

and knew about such things, thought that Custer sounded as if he was talking about a fox hunt.

"Ready when you are, George," Barnum said. "Good morning, Libbie."

"P., T.," she said, with a nod. "And good morning, Mr. Adams."

"Good morning, Mrs. Custer."

"Oh, please," she said, "I would very much like it if you would call me Libbie, Clint."

"All right, Libbie. I hope you've brought some of that pie along."

She smiled and said, "It's in the supply wagon, Clint, and I won't give away a piece until you've had one."

"Bless you."

Custer walked over to where his horse was, the reins being held by Major North. He mounted, then turned in the saddle to look back at his men, who all sat ramrod straight in their saddles.

The man who looked like either a scout or a buffalo hunter came over to Clint, Barnum and the rest and said, "Gentlemen, my name is Mickey Walls. You'll all be riding with me, so I'll be leading the way. It was my job to find a herd, and I did. It's the job of the platoon to keep the Indians off us, and I trust that they will."

"Are you a scout, Mr. Walls?" Barnum asked. "Or an actual buffalo hunter?"

"Well, sir," Walls said, "I've done lots of both, but I'm paid by the Army to be a scout."

"I see."

"The platoon will split into two columns," Walls explained. "One will move out first, and then we'll go. The second column will bring up the rear. I'll ask you all to stick to some kind of a formation and remain behind me.

Don't go wandering off because there are Indians out there. We are under the protection of the platoon. Do you understand all of this?"

The Easterners nodded and Barnum said, "I think we have a firm grasp on it, Mr. Walls."

"Good." Walls looked at Clint. "Mr. Adams, since you ain't an Easterner like the rest, I'd like you to ride with me."

"Whatever you say, Mr. Walls."

"Thank you."

Walls had sounded remarkably educated until he'd used the word "ain't." Now Clint was thinking that the man had somehow educated himself but was unable to keep his background from coming out from time to time.

"Are we ready, Mr. Walls?" Custer shouted.

"We're ready, sir!"

"First column, forward . . . ho!"

The first group of twenty-five troopers followed Custer as he rode toward the front gates and then out. Major North rode back to take his place at the head of the second column.

"Okay," Walls shouted, less formally, "let's move out!"

Clint rode alongside him, with Barnum right behind and the rest stretched out behind him. Finally, the second column of soldiers brought up the rear, and they were all on their way to the hunt.

TWENTY-THREE

The ride to the campsite was uneventful. Clint noticed that Mickey Walls was very alert, keeping a sharp eye all around them. He looked around himself but was unable to see anything. At the moment it didn't seem as if they were being watched.

When they reached the site, Custer immediately had his men make camp. The first thing they did was erect the tent that he and his wife would use as private quarters. After that, several campfires were set up, and men were given their watch assignments.

To Clint's surprise, a second, smaller tent was erected for the use of the Easterners, all of whom would probably have fit when they were all ready to turn in for the evening, but not if they were going to do any moving around.

Mickey Walls, though paid by the Army, was a ci-

vilian and as such was not billeted with the platoon. In
the end he and Clint staked out a spot around one of the
campfires, away from the Custer tent, and not far from
the Easterner's tent.

"We won't be doing any hunting until morning,"
Walls had told the Easterners, "so just get yourselves
situated and comfortable for the night."

They had ridden most of the day, but there was still
plenty of daylight left, a fact that did not escape the
notice of the Eastern party.

"Why can't we go out today?" Mayor Barker asked.

"I have to take a short ride and locate the herd," Walls
said. "I'm sure they're not going to be where I left them,
but I won't know how far they've moved until I take a
look."

"If you don't mind," Clint said, "I'll come along with
you."

"I don't mind at all," Walls said. "I'd enjoy the company."

"May I come along, too?" Barnum asked.

"I don't think that would be a very good idea, sir,"
Walls said. "Mr. Adams is experienced, and me and him
can watch out for ourselves. If we took you along we'd
have to watch out for you. Doing that, we might miss
something that would get us all killed."

"You wouldn't want that to happen, P. T., would
you?" Clint asked.

"No," Barnum said, "you're right about that. Very
well, I'll sit around here and twiddle my thumbs.
Shouldn't be so different from the rest of my retirement."

After the offer from Barnum the night before, Clint
knew the man's retirement was chafing him. This remark

only served to reinforce that. Barnum was just *itching* to burst out of retirement, but he needed a reason that would be good enough not only for him, but for his wife as well.

Walls said to Clint, "I'll just go and let the general know that you're coming with me and we can be off."

"Suits me."

Clint and Walls had not unsaddled their horses. Walls knew he was going to ride out of camp. Clint figured that Walls was going to and knew he was going to ask to go along. The only thing he hadn't been sure of was whether or not Walls would say yes.

"You been hunting before," Walls said. It was a statement, not a question.

"Yes," Clint answered. "I came here to hunt with a friend of mine, but he didn't show up."

"Mind if I ask who?"

"Bat Masterson."

"No kidding?"

Walls didn't seem impressed, just curious.

"No kidding."

"I hunted with Bat once."

"No kidding?" Clint asked.

Walls smiled and said, "No kidding."

He was a small man, five-seven or -eight, and built wide and strong. He looked to be in his mid-thirties, had piercing blue eyes and long, unruly hair. He and Custer were both wearing buckskin jackets, but Walls's had seen better days. It was "broken in."

He wore a gun, but he wore his gunbelt high, so Clint had a feeling he was better with a rifle.

"You're right," Walls said.

"About what?"

"I'm better with a rifle."

"You a mind reader, too?"

"Saw you lookin' at my handgun. You were thinkin' I wear it kinda high."

Now that they were alone, Walls's speech pattern had changed a bit. It was more natural. He wasn't being so careful about his choice of words.

"You're right."

"I can hit a gnat on a buffalo's ass on the run with my rifle," Walls said. "No brag, just fact."

"I believe you."

"That one time I hunted with Bat? He talked about you, some."

"That a fact?"

"Said you were the best man with a handgun he ever saw."

"That was nice of him."

"Also said he wouldn't rather have any other man covering his back."

"I feel the same way."

"Said you and he and Wyatt Earp used to hunt together."

"That was some time ago," Clint said.

They were approaching a rise, and Walls reined his horse in.

"The last I saw the herd they were over that rise."

"Why are we stopping then?"

"Because when I saw them there were some Indians there, too. Cheyenne."

"So we don't know what's over that rise right now."

"Not exactly."
"So I guess we'd better mind how we go."
Walls smiled.
"That's exactly what I was gonna say."

TWENTY-FOUR

They left their horses at the bottom of the rise and grounded their reins so they wouldn't run off. If there were Indians on the other side, the last thing they wanted was to be caught afoot.

As they approached the top of the rise, they got down on their bellies and crept the rest of the way. When they finally got to the top and looked down they saw . . . nothing.

"The herd's moved," Walls said.

"But you expected that."

"Yeah." Walls stood up, and Clint followed. "I just didn't know what else to expect. Let's get the horses and ride on down there. We can pick up their trail fairly easily."

They went back down to where they had left their horses. The rode them up the rise and down the other side. When they got to the bottom they could see that the ground had been churned up by many buffalo.

"Should we follow the trail?" Clint asked.

"Wait," Walls said. "I want to see if there are any other tracks."

"You mean Indians? How can you tell?"

"Come with me."

Walls rode through the churned up ground until he reached the other side. There they dismounted and he showed Clint the tracks made by Indian ponies as the braves rode alongside the big herd.

"How many?" he asked.

"Half a dozen, at least."

"No danger to our party, then."

"No," Walls said, "but a danger to us if we run into them."

They mounted up again.

"Okay, let's follow 'em and see how far they got," Walls said. "If they went too far we'll have to pull up the camp and move it."

The camp had looked pretty well set up when they left it. Clint knew that if they had to move it Custer wouldn't be happy.

He rode along with Walls, glad that the man had let him come along. He was a little older than Clint, and he felt that he was learning something from him.

"Okay, they split them up here. See the tracks?"

"Why'd they do that?"

"The Indians would pick out the ones they wanted and cut them out of the herd. Then they'd let the rest of the herd go on and move theirs along someplace where they could butcher them."

"Will we run across the carcasses?"

"There won't be much left. The Indians use as much of it as they can. That's why they hate the whites. We put more value on the coats than we do the meat, and we let the meat rot. They consider that a sinful waste."

Clint had hunted before, but he'd never run across a carcass left behind by Indians. But he knew they weren't going to see any today, because their job was to follow the main herd and see how far they'd gotten.

They moved on.

"There they are," Walls said.

From a distance away they could see the herd.

"Luckily we're downwind of them," he said. "They don't smell us, or our horses."

"They didn't go very far. What? A few miles? Must have been days ago when you were out here."

"Buffalo are very lazy animals," Walls said. "They really don't move much unless they're forced to. The Indians stopped driving them about a mile back and they settled in here."

"Doesn't look like they're going anywhere, either."

Many of the herd were on the ground, relaxing, or simply standing around, their heads lolling.

"We can go back," Walls said. "They're gonna be here for a while—until tomorrow for sure."

They wheeled their horses around and stopped short. A few hundred yards away six Indian braves sat on their ponies, watching them.

"Shit," Mickey Walls said.

TWENTY-FIVE

"What do we do now?" Clint asked.

"Just sit tight," Walls said, "and don't make any sudden moves."

"Why are they just watching us?"

"They don't know we're with the Army," Walls said. "We got no uniforms, and we're riding our own horses, not Army issue. There ain't anything Army issue about us. That's keepin' us alive, for now."

"I don't see any rifles," Clint said.

"That's good," Walls said. "Means we'll have them outgunned, if it comes to that."

They watched the Indians for a few moments and then Clint said, "They're just sitting there."

"They want to see what we'll do," Walls said. "If we make a run for it they'll chase us for sure."

"Well then, I suggest we keep that as an option."

"Agreed."

"So what do we do in the meantime."

Walls turned and looked behind them.

"We never made a move toward the herd," he said. "That's probably in our favor."

"Why don't we just start riding toward them slowly?" Clint suggested.

Walls turned his head to look at Clint, then looked back at the braves, who hadn't moved. They could have been looking at a painting of six Indians.

"We do have to go back that way to get back to camp," Walls said, "but what if they follow us? They'll find out we're Army."

"They'll also see fifty troops," Clint said. "I don't think they'd come anywhere near camp."

"They might come back with help, though."

"Look," Clint said, "I don't really know what's been going on in this region with the Indians lately."

"It's been quiet since Custer was assigned," Walls said. "They have special names for him."

Clint wasn't at all surprised, but neither was he the least bit curious what those names were.

"If they follow us back to camp they'll see Custer," Clint said. "If they respect him they'll stay away."

"You're probably right," Walls said, "but all of that doesn't do us any good right now. We've got to make a move before they do."

"Why not wait for them to move?"

"Because," Walls said, "Indians have more patience than white men. We could be here for days."

"Okay, then," Clint said, "let's ride right for them, make them move to let us by. That'll earn respect."

"Or get us killed."

"Either way," Clint said, "we'll be making the first move."

"Well," Walls said, "I don't have any other suggestions, so let's do it."

TWENTY-SIX

They started riding toward the braves, their hands holding their reins high to show that they weren't anywhere near their guns.

"We could probably take them, you know," Clint said.

"I'm not a gunman like you, Clint," Walls said. "Besides, they're just as accurate with their bows as we would with our guns. And remember, I'm better with a rifle, so don't count on me when it comes to gunplay with a handgun. Let's just ride and see what happens."

"Okay, fine," Clint said. Walls had to make the call. Clint couldn't, precisely because he didn't know how well Walls would hold up in a fight. He tried never to put his life in another man's hands when he didn't know how good those hands were.

The braves still hadn't moved as Clint and Walls

came closer and closer to them. Their ponies were standing remarkably still.

"Are they Cheyenne?"

"A lot of the Cheyenne have been captured," Walls said. "These look like Sioux to me."

"How have the Sioux been acting lately?"

"Quiet," Walls said, "which is exactly how these six are acting right now, ain't it?"

"Too quiet," Clint said. "I wish one of their ponies would even swish its tail."

But that didn't happen. As they got closer, though, it was as if God decided to toss Clint a bone. One of the ponies' left ear was twitching, probably because of a fly. In any case, *something* was moving.

As they got closer they saw that all six braves were young. That made it more amazing that they were so quiet and still.

"Many of the younger braves have been wanting to go on the offensive," Walls explained. "The older chiefs have been holding them off."

"Well, it doesn't look like there's an older chief in sight," Clint said.

"This may be good, though," Walls said. "There may only be these six and no others."

Finally, they were close enough that Clint and Walls could see the eyes of the Sioux warriors, and the Indians could also see theirs.

"No fear," Walls said.

"Easier said than done."

"You can feel it," Walls said, "but don't let it show."

Clint and Walls reached the Sioux and stopped. Rather than ride around them they stopped and faced them. They stared at each other for what seemed like days. Clint felt beads of sweat running down the small of his back. One even dropped off the tip of his nose, but he didn't move.

Finally, grudgingly, one of the braves nudged his horse and moved aside, The other five followed until there were three on each side. Clint let Walls go first, and they rode single file right through the six braves.

Now came the hard part. They had to keep riding and not look back, because looking back might show a sign of fear.

"Don't turn around," Walls said.

"I'm not."

They rode . . . and rode . . . and rode, slowly, never rushing their horses, just moving along at a nice, easy pace.

"Okay," Walls said, "let's turn to the east just a bit so we can look back. It won't look like we're turning around."

"Right."

They both moved their reins and turned their horses to the left. Just by moving their heads slightly they were able to look back . . . and see that the Indians were gone.

"Keep moving," Walls said. "We don't know where they are."

"Maybe," Clint said, "they didn't even watch us. They just left after we passed them."

"Did you hear their horses move?" Walls asked.

"No."

"Neither did I. They're like ghosts."

Clint looked at Walls for the first time.

"That was something."

"Don't know that I coulda done that with another

man, Adams," Walls said. "Sure as hell nobody else in camp."

"Thanks."

"We got to thank each other," Walls said. "The slightest show of fear or panic on either part and we both might have been dead."

"You know what?" Clint asked.

"What?"

"I think we can ride faster now."

"I agree," Walls said, and they each kicked their horses into full gallop.

TWENTY-SEVEN

They rode into camp that way, attracting everyone's interest. Walls saved his report for Custer, though, and Clint went along to corroborate it, if the need arose. He was satisfied, though, to see that Custer treated Walls with some respect.

"Six Sioux braves?" Custer asked. "That's all you saw?"

"Yes, sir," Walls said, "and they were young bucks, General, so I think they're on their own."

Custer looked at Clint who, for a moment, thought he was going to be asked his opinion, but then the general looked back to his scout.

"And what about the buffalo?"

"We found 'em, sir," Walls said, "a whole herd. Looks like those braves cut the ones they wanted from the herd earlier."

"How far away are they?"

"Coupla miles, is all."

"No need to break camp and move it?"

"No, sir," Walls said. "We can get to them easy enough."

"All right, Mr. Walls," Custer said. "Thank you for your report. Get yourself something to eat."

"Yes, sir."

He turned to leave and Clint turned with him.

"Mr. Adams, would you stay a moment?"

"Sure, General."

Walls continued out of the tent. Clint wondered where Libbie Custer was. Custer had a field desk set up in the tent and was sitting behind it. It was then Clint realized that the tent had two compartments. Libbie must have been in the other one, where they would sleep.

"What did you think of Mr. Walls, Mr. Adams?"

"He's a helluva a good man, General," Clint said. "Smart, competent, brave. We could have easily gotten killed out there if he hadn't kept his head."

"And you yours, I have no doubt."

"We worked together well."

"I realize that," Custer said, "which is why I am going to offer you a job, sir."

Yep, Clint thought, everybody was offering him a job these days. Did he look like he needed a job?

"General—"

"Now hear me out, sir," Custer said. "It wouldn't be me you'd be working for, but the government."

"All right, sir. I'll hear you out."

"Mr. Walls is very valuable to me," Custer said, "as I am sure you would be. I need two men who can work together and watch each others' backs. You have proven to me that you and Mr. Walls can do that."

"General," Clint said, "Mickey Walls's business is scouting, mine is not. In fact, I'm not even sure what my business is. All I am sure or if is that since I arrived here I've received three job offers."

"Indeed?" Custer asked. "And which do you intend to take?"

"With all due respect, to you and to the U.S. Government, General, I don't intend to take any. I assumed I was invited to hunt with you. I took that as an honor and accepted. When this hunt is over I intend to move on, almost immediately."

"What were the other jobs?" Custer asked. "Or would you rather not say?"

Clint hesitated just a moment, then saw no harm in answering the question honestly.

"Fred and Kate Hooper have offered me a job working in their saloon," Clint said, "and P. T. Barnum has offered me a job."

"And what would they have you do?"

"They both want the same thing," Clint said, realizing it at that precise moment.

"And what is that?"

"They want to put me on display for the purposes of making money."

"The government does not want to do that," Custer said. "We want to pay you to do the things you do best."

"I do the things I do best because I want to, General, not because I have to," Clint said. "I'm afraid my answer still has to be no."

Custer—just as Barnum had done before him—said, "Think it over and give me an answer after the hunt."

"I'll think it over, General," Clint said, "but I'm afraid my answer will be the same."

Custer smiled a humorless smile and said, "We'll see. That's all."

Clint knew he'd been dismissed, was tempted to stand his ground and leave when he was ready, but he decided that would be childish. He turned and left the tent. Outside he found Mickey Walls standing nearby.

"Did you hear?" he asked.

"I heard," Walls said. "If I was you I'd take the job with Barnum. At least he'd be making money for you, too."

"I would be making money for the both of us," Clint said. "Look, I'm sorry, Mickey, I know how important it is to have someone watch your back—"

Walls held up his hand and stopped Clint cold.

"Don't apologize to me," Walls said. "I been staying alive very nicely on my own. You do what you got to do."

"No hard feelings?"

"None," Walls said, then smiled and said, "Well, hardly any."

The two men laughed and shook hands.

"I'll see to both horses," Walls said.

"Thanks."

"See you at the fire."

Clint waved, turned and walked toward the biggest fire, where he'd be able to get some coffee.

TWENTY-EIGHT

Clint was hunkered down by the fire with a cup of coffee in his hand when Barnum came walking over.

"You mind if I ask what that was all about?"

"What what was all about?"

"Well," the showman said, helping himself to a cup of coffee, "you came riding in here like something was chasing you."

"We found the herd," Clint said, "and saw some Indians."

Barnum stopped with his cup halfway to his mouth.

"*Saw* some Indians?" he asked. "Did you *engage* them?"

"No," Clint said, "we just rode right through them, and they disappeared."

"How many of them?"

"Six."

"Were they painted with war paint and carrying guns?" Barnum asked, excitedly.

"No on both counts, P. T.," Clint said. "They were a peaceful hunting party, and we just happened to cross paths with them. That's all."

"So we're still going to be hunting tomorrow morning?"

"Definitely."

"Excuse me, gentlemen," Major North said, interrupting them.

Clint and Barnum stood up and faced the second in command.

"Mrs. Custer requests your company for dinner, outside of the general's tent," North said.

"Tell Mrs. Custer I'll be there," Clint said.

"And I," Barnum chimed in.

"One half hour, then, gentlemen."

"See you then," Barnum said, and Clint nodded.

As the major walked away, Barnum looked around the camp and asked, "Is this how buffalo hunts usually go?"

"Well, so far," Clint said, "I've never been on one like this before. Usually there's no tents, and we're all just sleeping in our bedrolls."

"Well, I suppose we'll be sleeping on the ground while we're here," Barnum said, "but I do like the idea of being in a tent."

Clint studied the man for a moment. The showman had probably been to every major country in Europe, stayed in the finest hotels, slept in the softest—or firmest—beds, and met many heads of state. Clint really couldn't understand why he'd want to be out here sleeping on the ground, in or out of a tent.

"Do you suppose the major meant for me to bring the others to dinner?" Barnum asked.

"I think we should leave it to Mrs. Custer and the major to extend the invitations."

"Good idea. I'll see you at dinner, then."

"See you then."

Barnum set down his cup and walked away. Clint poured himself more coffee and willed himself to relax for the half an hour before dinner. He really hadn't taken a deep breath since riding into camp and going with Walls to report to Custer. He sat back and took the deep breath now, then let it out slowly. Maybe accepting the invitation to come on this hunt had been a bad idea. He might have been better off just riding out after he found that Bat wasn't coming.

He looked around the camp, at the soldiers and the Easterners, over at Custer's tent, outside of which a table was being set for dinner. This certainly was like no camp he'd ever been in before.

He could only wonder what tomorrow held for them.

Right on time Clint walked over to Custer's tent and was greeted warmly by Libbie Custer. Behind him came the other invitees, Barnum and K. C. Barker. Apparently the other men in the Eastern party had not received the same invitation.

Libbie was setting the table herself, having left Eliza behind. Actually, she was not doing it herself—she had a young private helping her.

"Please, all of you, be seated," she said. Clint guessed that the table and chairs had been on the chuck wagon that had followed behind them. He could see the army cook serving the men their dinner over by the bigger fire and felt that he would rather be over there than here at the Custer's table.

Except maybe for Libbie Custer's pie.

"Private, you may go and fetch the general," she said.

"Yes, Ma'am."

The private went to the tent and informed the general that dinner was ready. Custer came out and greeted his guests magnanimously, seating himself among them.

Libbie and the private served the dinner, which appeared to be leftovers from the previous night—cold chicken, vegetables and biscuits and, for later, some pie. Once Libbie was ready to seat herself, she told the private to go and have his own supper but be back in half an hour.

Major North came along then, the last to join them. Clint had wondered if Mickey Walls was going to join them. The obvious answer was no.

"P. T., you'll be happy to know that Clint and my man, Mr. Walls, located the herd for us. They're only a couple of miles from here, and they did not look like they'd be moving anytime soon."

"Capital!" K. C. Barker said. "I can't wait to get my first buffalo."

Clint thought that if the herd were as lazy as they looked, Barker was going to get his first one and a lot more.

"Clint mentioned something about Indians, George."

Custer gave Clint a disapproving look, which he ignored.

"Just a small hunting party, Phineas," Custer assured him. "Nothing to worry about."

"I'm not worried," Barnum said. "I'd love to see them."

"We may and we may not," Custer said. "That's not something we can arrange, Phineas. The Indians don't really cooperate with us."

"Too bad."

"I don't know why you'd want to see them, P. T.," Libbie Custer said. "They're such . . . filthy animals."

"I'd just like to see that for myself, Miss Libbie," Barnum said. "I'm a man who likes to see things for myself."

"P. T. probably wants to make them an offer to put them on display," Barker said. "Like one of his oddities. He could make them famous." Barker laughed. "You think they'd respond to that kind of an offer, P. T.?"

"Who knows, K. C.," Barnum said, "who knows?"

"Or maybe you'd like to put Mr. Adams on display," Barker went on. "Why don't you make him an offer?"

"It's my understanding that such an offer has already been made," Custer said, "and turned down."

Custer seemed self-satisfied as he revealed this, as if it was his way of getting back at Clint for telling Barnum about the Indians.

"Is that true, P. T.?" Barker asked. "Mr. Adams turned you down?"

Barnum looked at Clint, who did not respond, so the showman said, "I'm afraid that's between Mr. Adams and myself, K. C."

Barnum bent to the task of eating dinner and would not discuss the matter further, which suited Clint just fine.

TWENTY-NINE

This dinner was different from the one the night before. Instead of Barnum and Clint regaling the diners with stories, it was Custer who talked and everyone else who listened. At one point, Clint caught Libbie's eye and he thought that she winked at him and shrugged, although he couldn't be sure.

Custer talked for hours, until Libbie was finally the one who excused herself and went into the tent to go to sleep. Apparently, it would be up to the private to clean everything up alone.

After Libbie left, Custer broke out cigars and passed them around.

"Let's take a walk," he said, standing.

"With Indians out there?" Barker asked.

"A small party, Mr. Barker," Custer said, "and I assure you they will come nowhere near this camp. Be-

135

sides, the night air will do you good. It will help you to sleep."

"I'm for a walk," Barnum said. "Clint?"

"Sure," Clint said, "why not?"

"Well," Barker said, "I won't stay behind."

Custer turned to the private and said, "You can break everything down, son."

"Yes, sir."

Custer walked ahead, and Barker hurried to catch up, apparently feeling safer with the general.

"I'm not going to need any help sleeping," Barnum said. "Not after all that."

"Did you ever think of putting Custer on display?" Clint asked.

"He'd put an audience to sleep," Barnum said. "On the other hand, you wouldn't."

"I already gave you my answer, P. T."

"I know, I know," Barnum said, "but that doesn't mean I have to give up trying, does it?"

"I wish you would," Clint said. "I wish everybody would."

"You're in demand right now?"

"Even Custer offered me a job working for the Army—or for him."

"Neither one appeals to you?"

"No."

"Do you think you'll ever get tired of just travelling around, Clint? Maybe settle down someplace?"

"Maybe," Clint admitted, "but not for a long, long time."

"Well," Barnum said, "if it's in my lifetime, make sure you come and see me. My offer is a standing one."

"I'll keep that in kind, P. T."

They followed Custer around for a while as he continued to regale K. C. and Barnum with stories of Indian fighting, and eventually they worked their way back to camp.

"Well, you were right, George," Barnum said. "I'm ready to turn in. That night air really did it."

"Me, too," Barker said. "Goodnight, all."

"Goodnight, Clint," Barnum said.

"Goodnight, P. T."

The two men walked off to their tent, and Custer turned to Clint.

"Is he still trying to put you on display?"

"Still trying."

"He's asked me many times," Custer said, which Clint knew was a lie, "but I keep turning him down. When I'm ready to tell my story, I'll do it in a published memoir. Publishers are already after me."

"That should be very flattering."

"It is, it is," Custer said. "Well, I'll be turning in as well. You will, uh, continue to consider my offer, won't you?"

"I'll think it over, General," Clint said.

"That's all I ask," Custer said. "Goodnight."

Clint watched Custer until he had gone into his tent and then walked over to the fire he was sharing with Mickey Walls. The scout was already wrapped in his bedroll but turned his head as Clint approached.

"How was dinner?"

"Boring."

"Wait until tomorrow," Walls said. "If we don't put some life into that herd, it will be the most boring buffalo hunt in history."

"You don't think they'll run when the shooting starts?"

"If I'm any judge of buffalo," Walls said, "tomorrow is going to be a slaughter."

Suddenly, as he wrapped himself in his bedroll, Clint was dead sure that coming on this hunt had been a mistake.

THIRTY

And it was a slaughter.

Early the next morning, Custer, P. T. Barnum, K. C. Barker, Major North, Clint and the rest of Barker's party, plus thirty troopers, rode out to find the herd. The other troopers remained behind to guard the camp and Mrs. Custer. Mickey Walls led the group, who were rowdy and ready to shoot some buffalo.

When they reached the point where they had seen the herd the day before, it was still there. The buffalo were still lolling about lazily.

"How do you want to do this, General?" Walls asked. "Do you want to shoot from here or ride up on them? You want me to get them moving?"

"Do you think you can?" Custer said. "They looked as if they couldn't move if they tried."

"I can find out," Walls said. "Just have your guns ready when they start to run."

"We'll be ready," Custer said.

"Why make them move?" one of the men asked.

"Won't we have to chase them?" another chimed in.

"Hunting buffalo from horseback is a rare pleasure, gentlemen," Custer informed them.

"Yeah, but what if we, you know, fall off our horse?" a third man asked. "Won't we be trampled?"

"I'd advise you not to fall off your horse," Custer said, with disdain. "P. T.? You want to shoot them from here?"

"It's your hunt, George," Barnum said. "I'm your guest. However you want to do this is fine with me."

"Let's see if Mr. Walls can get them moving."

The next few minutes amazed Clint. Walls rode up on the herd, which should have been enough to get them stirring. They didn't move or acknowledge him. He rode his horse around them, and then in among them. Finally, he rode away from them, took out his rifle and fired a few shots.

They didn't budge.

"Well," Custer said, "looks like we found ourselves a lazy herd." He turned to look at Barker. "You and your friends can shoot from here, or ride down on them and take your pick, and it seems you won't have to worry about being trampled."

"You heard the man," Barker said. "Let's hunt buffalo."

Clint had seen this kind of slaughter only once before, and it had sickened him then. He watched as Barker and his men rode to the herd, passing Walls as he rode back.

When they reached the herd they began firing into it, and buffalo began to die.

"Jesus," P. T. said.

"Phineas?" Custer asked. "Don't you want to join in?"

Barnum swallowed as he watched his friends slaughter buffalo. Custer eventually rode up on the buffalo and began firing himself. Walls and Major North remained with Clint and Barnum. The troopers watched with no expression on any of their faces.

"They're killing so many," he said. "Why so many?"

"You couldn't stop them now if you tried," Clint said. "I've seen this kind of blood lust before."

"Why don't they run?" Barnum demanded.

"Damndest thing I ever saw," Walls said, shaking his head. "Major?"

"Never saw the like before, Mr. Walls."

Walls looked at Clint.

"Once, many years ago," Clint said. "It almost put me off buffalo hunting for good."

"My God," Barnum said, "it *has* put me off it. Major?"

"Sir?"

"Can you have someone take me back to camp? I have no desire to watch this any further."

"I'll take you back," Clint said.

Walls looked at both of them and said, "I wish I could go with you."

"I can send five men to escort you back," North said, "but no more."

"That's fine, Major," Clint said. "I'll leave that decision to you. I can find the way."

"You're both guests of the United States Army,"

North said. "If you get killed, it's my ass."

"All right," Clint said, "five men it is."

"And could you pick them out fast?" Barnum asked, looking as if he was going to puke.

THIRTY-ONE

When they got back to camp, Barnum went immediately to his tent. The five troopers who had escorted them back rode out again to rejoin the others. Clint took care of his horse and Barnum's. As he was doing so, Mrs. Custer came walking over to him.

"Has something happened?" she asked.

He turned to face her and removed his hat.

"Mr. Barnum has lost his taste for buffalo hunting, Ma'am."

"And you?"

"What I saw out there was not hunting, Mrs. Custer," he said, "it was out and out slaughter."

"And my husband?"

"He's still out there with the others."

"Will you be going back the fort, then?"

143

"I imagine Mr. Barnum will want to."

"Good," she asked. "May I accompany you?"

"I don't know if that would be a very good idea, Mrs. Custer."

"I thought you were going to call me Libbie."

"The general wouldn't be too happy about you leaving, would he, Libbie?" Clint asked.

"Probably not," she said, "but I'm a grown woman and make my own decisions. If you are going back to the fort, I would like to ride along."

"Why don't we see what P. T. has to say?" Clint asked. "If he wants to go back, then I don't see any reason why you couldn't tag along."

At that moment, Barnum came out of his tent carrying his rifle and bedroll.

"Just point me in the direction of the fort," he said.

"Nonsense, P. T.," Clint said. "I'll take you back."

"I'll have a few men ride back with us," Libbie said.

"Can you do that?" Clint asked.

"I'm the general's wife," she said. "They won't refuse me."

Clint wondered why she hadn't just gotten a few men to take her back already. Why did she have to wait for him? This was not going to make him very popular with Custer.

"I'll be ready in a few minutes," she said and hurried away.

"She's leaving, too?" Barnum asked.

"It looks that way. Are you all right?"

"That was the most horrible thing I've ever seen," Barnum said.

"It was pretty bad."

"I don't believe the others could take part in it and not feel sick."

"Oh," Clint said, "they'll feel sick, all right. When it's all over and they've seen what they've done, they'll feel it."

"And George?"

"I have the feeling the general knows exactly what he's doing at all times," Clint said, "or thinks he does."

Barnum shook his head and went to tie his bedroll to his horse.

Libbie Custer appeared moments later with a horse, rather than with the buggy that had taken her out there. The three of them, along with three troopers who didn't know if they were going to have their heads handed to them or not, rode out of camp and headed back to Fort Hays.

When they reached the fort, Libbie dismounted and turned to Clint.

"Thank you for bringing me back, Mr. Adams."

"It was my pleasure, Libbie."

"Will you be leaving Hays City?"

"First thing in the morning."

"It was a pleasure to have met you," Libbie said. "And P. T.?"

"First stage I can get back, my dear, I'll be on it."

"Then it was a pleasure to meet you as well. I wish both of you gentlemen all the best."

They watched as she walked to her quarters and went inside. Barnum, riding an Army horse, left it behind. Clint walked him back to town with his horse trailing behind them.

"What do you suppose that was all about?" Barnum asked.

"Trouble in paradise, I guess," Clint said. "Sort of makes me glad I never got married."

"There is a lot to be said for marriage," Barnum said. "I have three beautiful daughters because of it."

"Guess I don't have any great urge to be a daddy."

"I don't know that I did, either," Barnum said. "I mean, I love my girls, but the only urge I've ever had was for the show business."

"Seems to me you've made the most of it."

"Not yet," Barnum said. "I haven't made all that I can of it."

They turned down the main street of Hays City and headed for their hotel.

"Does this mean you're coming out of retirement?"

"Just as soon as I get back to New York."

"Doing what?"

"I don't know," Barnum said, "something that will wipe this day out of my memory, I suppose."

When they reached the hotel they stopped, and Barnum gave him the same thanks Libbie had.

"Thanks for bringing me back."

"I'll be taking my horse to the livery," Clint said. "If I'm going to be leaving tomorrow, I'll have to make arrangements to buy it."

"Perhaps we'll see each other again," Barnum said.

"Probably before we leave town."

Barnum laughed.

"I meant after we leave here, Clint," Barnum said. "Keep my offer in mind. It's always open."

"I'll do that, P. T."

"Then I won't say good-bye," Barnum said. "I'll see you sometime in the future."

As Barnum went inside and Clint walked his horse to the livery, neither man realized that their next meeting would not be for almost fifteen years . . .

PART TWO
New York, years later

THIRTY-TWO

Felicity Parker very much enjoyed seeing the circus in Madison Square Garden. Clint Adams enjoyed it as well, but couldn't help wondering about P. T. Barnum. He had not seen Barnum since that last day in Hays City in 1870. Somehow, he managed to leave town the next morning without seeing the showman again. He did not, however, get away without seeing Savannah and Kate Hooper again. When he got to his room that night both were there waiting for him, naked, in his bed. He decided not to worry about whether or not Kate was married. Having both of them there was too much of a gift to question. It was one of those nights you still remember, years later.

"What are you thinking?" Felicity asked him, after the show was over.

"Hmm?"

"You have a grin on your face like the cat who ate the canary," she said.

"Do I? Sorry. We better get moving."

"Let's wait for most of the crowd to leave," she said. "I don't want to be shoved around."

Clint felt that he could have protected her from that, but decided to do as she asked.

"All right."

Barnum had to be in his late seventies now, he thought. He wondered what kind of shape the old showman was in.

"I was thinking . . ." Felicity said.

"About what?"

"Well," she said, excitedly, "since you know P. T. Barnum personally, I was wondering if you could get us in to see him?"

"Oh, I don't know," Clint said. "That was a long time ago, Felicity. He might not even remember me."

She hit him on the arm and said, "Stop. How could he not remember you? Everybody knows who you are."

"Well," he said, "hopefully not everybody."

"Come on," she said, "I'd love to meet him. They say he's brilliant."

"Do they?"

"Everyone says so!"

"Well," Clint said, "not everybody."

"Come on, Mr. Adams," she said, "you want to show a girl a good time, don't you?"

"I thought I'd done that already."

She grabbed his arm and yanked on it.

"Come on," she said. "If you get me in to meet P. T. Barnum, I'll show *you* a good time."

"I thought you'd already—"

"Clint!"

"All right," he said. "I'll see what I can do. Come on. We'll have to get down to the floor."

They followed the crowd down to the floor and then started trying to find their way to someone they could talk to, somebody who worked for the circus. They finally saw somebody wearing a uniform that indicated he was employed by the circus.

"Excuse me," Clint said to him, "I'd like to talk to someone about seeing P. T. Barnum."

"Yeah," the man said, "you and a lot of other people."

"I think if you tell him my name he'll see me."

"Mister," the man said, "I just work here. I don't get to see Mr. Barnum."

"Can you tell me who can help me?"

"You'll have to go to the main office, ask for the manager, a man named Bollinger, Andrew Bollinger."

"Bollinger," Clint said. "All right, thanks. How do I get to the office?"

The man gave him directions, and he and Felicity went off in search of it.

They found the Garden office at a far end of the building, but an armed guard was standing in front of it.

"Stop there!" the man said, with his hand on his holstered pistol. "You can't go any farther."

"We're looking for Mr. Barnum," Clint said, eyeing the man warily. He was not wearing his own holstered weapon but had his Colt New Line stuck in the back of his trousers, inside the belt.

"What's your business with him?"

"I'm a friend of his."

"Yeah, right," the guard said. "Mr. Barnum's got more friends than he knows what to do with."

"He really is an old friend," Felicity said. "Won't you please tell Mr. Barnum we're here?"

The man, in his forties and thick through his middle, eyed Felicity with appreciation.

"I can't do it, Miss—"

"Mr. Barnum is going to be very upset if you don't tell him his friend Clint Adams is here," she said in a scolding tone.

The guard immediately recognized the name. His eyebrows went up and he stared at Clint.

"Are you really Clint Adams?"

"He really is," Felicity said. "I wouldn't lie."

"And you really know Mr. Barnum?"

"I knew him years ago," Clint said. "I haven't seen him in some time."

The guard chewed his lip, stared at Clint, looked Felicity over again, then said, "Wait here."

He turned and went into the office. When he came out he had a young man with him.

"Mr. Adams?"

"That's right."

The man extended his hand and Clint grasped it.

"My name is Matthew Scott. I'm an assistant to Mr. Barnum."

"Is P. T. here?"

"He was," Scott said, "but we usually hustle him out of here very quickly, just before the finale, in order to get him safely through the crowd."

"Is that because of his, uh, age?"

Scott smiled.

"He'd laugh to hear you say that," the young man said. He looked to be in his late twenties. "No, Mr. Barnum can still get around pretty well on his own. It's because of the threats."

"What threats?"

"There have been some threats against Mr. Barnum's life. That's why we have private guards watching the office door. P. T. had a bodyguard, but he fired the man recently."

"Why was that?"

"They didn't get along," Scott said. "P. T. can still get around, but his patience is not what it once was."

"Who's threatening him?"

"Well," Scott said, "we believe the threats—excuse me, I'm sorry. I've forgotten my manners. Would you like to come into the office for a few minutes?"

"Yes, thank you," Clint said.

Scott opened the door and said. "Ma'am?" to Felicity, allowing her to precede him. As Clint went in ahead of him as well, he heard Scott say to the guard, "Thanks, Andy. You can go."

"Thanks, Mr. Scott. . . . Uh, is that really Clint Adams?"

"Well," Scott said, "to tell you the truth, Andy, I don't know. I've never seen the man. But I'm going to take him at his word, for now."

"Want me to stick around?"

"No," Scott said, "you go ahead."

"G'night, Mr. Scott."

" 'nighe, Andy."

Matthew Scott entered the office and closed the door

behind him, aware that Clint and Felicity were able to hear his conversation with the guard.

"As I told Andy, I'm going to assume you're telling the truth about who you are," he said to Clint.

"P. T. could tell you who I am."

"As I said, he's not here," Scott said. "His wife, Nancy, has taken him home."

"Nancy?"

"Oh, didn't you know? P. T. remarried after his first wife passed away. Nancy is . . . quite a bit younger than him. Forty years, in fact."

"Forty?" Felicity said, incredulously.

"Yes," Scott said, "but they're very much in love."

"Mr. Scott," Clint said, "maybe you're not sure about who I am, but will you tell me about the threats?"

"Well, we believe they originated with a man named Forepaugh, Adam Forepaugh. He's a . . . competitor of P. T.'s. Another showman. They're sort of . . . arguing over white elephants."

"What was that again?" Clint asked. "I'm not sure I heard you right."

"White elephants."

"That's what I thought you said."

"I can explain," Scott said, "but maybe P. T. would rather do that himself. If you tell me what hotel your staying in, I'll talk to P. T. and then get a message to you. If P. T. agrees, I'll set up an appointment for you to come to his home."

"All right," Clint said. "I'm at the Waldorf."

"Very good," Scott said.

"And when you speak to him," Clint said, "would you ask him if the lady may come, as well?"

"Yes, of course I will," Scott said. "Now suppose I show the two of you how to get out of here without braving the crowd, eh?"

THIRTY-THREE

Clint and Felicity caught a cab back to the Waldorf, where they were both staying.

"Why would someone threaten Mr. Barnum?" she asked. "I thought he was beloved in New York?"

"By everyone but his competition, I guess," Clint said. "I'm more curious about this white elephant stuff."

"Aren't you worried about your friend?"

"Everybody makes enemies, Felicity."

"I have none."

"That you know of."

"No, seriously," she said. "I have no enemies."

"Everybody loves you?"

"Well, I wouldn't go that far—"

"Don't you know some women who don't like you because you're more beautiful than they are?"

"Well, yes, I suppose—"

"And don't you think they might do something to you because of it."

She frowned.

"I don't like to think I have enemies," she said, "but there are some women—"

"And most of them probably just envy you," Clint said, "and would never do anything to hurt you. But there might be just that one—"

"You're going to help him, aren't you?"

"Who? P. T.? It sounds like he has plenty of help."

"But he fired his bodyguard."

"So? He'll hire another one."

"Yes," she said, "you."

"No, not me," Clint said. "He tried to get me to work for him once before, to put me on display—"

"But this would be different."

"If I agreed to work for him, in any capacity," Clint told her, "he'd find a way to exploit it and make money from it."

"That's not fair."

"Yes, it is," Clint said. "I know him well enough to know *that*."

"You knew him years ago. Are you the same man he knew then?"

"No, but—"

"Then maybe he's not the same man you knew then, either."

Clint paused a moment, then said, "You're right, Felicity. Maybe he's not the same man."

"Then you'll help him?"

"We don't even know that he'll ask—"

"But if he does?"

He hesitated again, then said, "We'll see."

• • •

Clint thought it very likely that they might never hear from Matthew Scott again. Maybe the man never did believe that he was Clint Adams and was only humoring him. Maybe he would not ever mention his visit to P. T. Barnum at all.

Clint was thinking about this in the dining room of the Waldorf, where he was having dinner with Felicity, when a bellhop entered, looked around, spotted him and hurried over.

"Message for you, Mr. Adams."

The bellhop handed him the message, and Clint took the time to tip the boy before he opened it.

"Is it from Barnum?" Felicity asked, excited.

"Yes, it is."

"What does it say?"

"It's an invitation to visit him at his home on Astor Place."

"Astor Place? How wonderful. When?"

"Tonight."

"Let's go," she said, starting to rise.

Clint held a hand out to stop her and said, "I'm sure P. T. can wait until I've finished my steak, Felicity."

"But what if—"

"It's a very good steak," Clint said. "I'm paying for it, and I would like to finish it."

"Fine," she said, sitting back down.

"How about finishing your dinner, too?"

"I'm finished," she said. "I'm too excited to eat."

"Well, I still have to have my pie and coffee—"

"Clint Adams! You are not going to make me wait while you eat pie and coffee. Finish your steak and then I demand that we go see P. T. Barnum."

If she had been standing she would have stamped her foot.

"Well," Clint said, cutting into his meat, "if you put it that way . . ."

After he had finally finished his steak, Felicity just about dragged him out in front of the hotel, where they asked the doorman to get them a cab. Once inside, Clint gave the man the address they wanted.

"That's P. T. Barnum's house," the driver said.

"How do you know that?" Clint asked.

"Every cabman in New York knows Barnum's house. You a friend of his, are you?"

"I am."

"Well, you just sit back and I'll have you there in two shakes."

"Everybody really does love P. T. Barnum, don't they?" Felicity asked.

"No," Clint reminded her, "not everyone."

THIRTY-FOUR

Clint got down from the cab and helped Felicity down. They turned to walk to the front door of P. T. Barnum's home and the door opened for them before they got there. Light flooded out and as they walked in Matthew Scott stepped out.

"I'm a man of my word, Mr. Adams," he said.

"Obviously."

"Come in, please," Scott said. "P. T. is waiting. Hello, Miss . . ."

"Parker," Clint said. "I'm sorry I didn't properly introduce her this afternoon. Miss Felicity Parker."

"Miss Parker," Scott said.

"Mr. Scott."

Scott closed the door, then indicated that Clint and Felicity should precede him.

"P. T. is in his office. It's that way."

The three of them walked down a hallway, and Scott stopped them in front of a solid oak door.

"Excuse me." He stepped past Felicity, knocked, and opened the door.

"P. T.? They're here."

"Well let them, young Mr. Scott, let them in." The voice was one that Clint didn't recognize, but he did recognize the phrasing as P. T. Barnum's.

Clint and Felicity entered, and P. T. rose from behind his oak desk. Standing next to him was a young lovely woman, no doubt the second Mrs. Barnum. She was blond, healthy looking, with a somewhat prominent chin but an amazing complexion.

Clint instantly recognized Barnum, even as he was surprised at the changes time had made in the man. No longer ramrod straight, Barnum stood slightly bent forward at the waste. The once impressive main of hair had been reduced and grayed, and his face was covered with lines and creases. But the smile remained, and the man's vitality was evident, even just standing in a small room behind his desk.

"Clint Adams," Barnum said, "by God, man."

Barnum put his hand out, and Clint moved forward to take it. The grasp was firm, but not strong.

"Hello, P. T."

"Come to take me up on my offer, I hope?"

"Still think you could make money putting me on display?"

"Millions more than I ever thought," Barnum said. "More than I've made with Jumbo. You've come a long, long way. This is my wife, Nancy."

"Mrs. Barnum," Clint said.

"Oh, please call me Nancy," she said, "and I hope I may call you Clint?"

"Please do. This is my friend, Felicity Parker. She has been very anxious to meet you, P. T."

"Ah, Miss Parker," Barnum said, putting out his hand. Felicity rushed forward to place her hand in his.

"It's an honor, Mr. Barnum."

"The honor is mine, my dear, I assure you. Matthew, chairs for out guests?"

"Silas is bringing them—ah, here they are."

A black man entered carrying two extra chairs.

"Thank you, Silas," Nancy said.

"Yes, Mum."

Nancy arranged the chairs in front of Barnum's desk, one each for Clint, Felicity and Matthew Scott. There was already a chair on the other side of the desk, next to Barnum's. Clint was surprised to see that Barnum needed the arm of his wife in order to sit down. Her did so with a great sigh of relief.

Barnum looked up and saw the look on Clint's face.

"Yes, yes," he said, "the body is weak, but the mind is still as sharp as ever."

"I don't doubt that, P. T.," Clint said. "Not for a minute."

"Drinks, Matthew?"

"Brandy, Miss Parker?" Scott said, getting to his feet.

"Yes, please."

"Mr. Adams?"

"I don't think—"

"Please, have one, Clint," Barnum said. "This is the only way I get to enjoy good brandy, by watching others drink it."

"All right."

They all waited while Scott poured drinks for everyone but Barnum. That done, Scott seated himself again, next to Felicity.

"So what's it been, Clint? Fifteen years since Hays City?"

"At least."

"Poor George, eh?" Barnum said. "Little Big Horn must have been a great shock to him."

"It was a shock to most people," Clint said, "but probably not to Custer. He must have known how outmanned he'd be."

"Then you're saying he was foolish? And deserved to die?"

"No one deserves to die like that," Clint said, "especially not the men who followed him."

"And you wouldn't have?"

"No."

"They had their orders."

"Their orders were insane . . ."

"And Custer?"

Clint hesitated, then said, "I didn't come here to discuss Custer or the Little Big Horn."

"No, of course not," Barnum said, "nor to accept my fifteen-year-old offer, I'll wager."

"No."

"Still object to being out on display for money?"

"Yes."

"Still refreshingly candid, aren't you?"

Clint smiled at that and said, "Yes."

"Well, I know why you're here."

"Do you?"

"Of course," Barnum said. "Scott brought you. He thinks I need your help."

"I know you do, P. T.," Scott said.

"I actually came because Felicity wanted to meet you."

"Not to see an old friend?"

"Do you want me to be refreshingly candid again, P. T.?"

The old man laughed, and the laugh turned into a coughing fit. He bent at the waist, as if every cough caused him pain, and Nancy bent to him solicitously, soothing him. Clint looked at Scott, who shook his head slightly.

Eventually the cough subsided. Nancy went to the same sideboard Scott had gotten the brandy from and brought her husband a glass of water. Her movements, and the concern etched on her face, and the gentleness with which she touched her much older husband convinced Clint that she was very much in love with him.

"I'm sorry," Barnum said. "Sometimes I can't . . . well, I'm sorry."

"That's all right."

"Where were we?"

"My reason for being here."

"Hmm," Barnum said, then looked at his wife. "Nancy, why don't you take Felicity and show her the house, hmm?"

"Will you be all right?"

"Yes, yes," Barnum said, "I'll be fine. Scott is here."

Nancy looked at Felicity with a smile and said, "Come, my dear, they want us to be gone."

It was odd the way she called Felicity "my dear," for

Nancy was obviously the younger of the two.

Felicity gave in without argument and followed Nancy from the room. None of the men spoke again until the door closed behind the two ladies.

"What's all this about a white elephant?" Clint asked.

THIRTY-FIVE

"You heard about the white elephant?" Barnum asked.

"Uh, I told him, P. T."

"And about Forepaugh?"

"Yes," Clint said. "Have you any proof that he's behind the threats?"

"I don't need proof."

"The law does."

"The law isn't doing anything about it."

"He did have a bodyguard," Scott said, "but he fired him."

"He was incompetent."

"What about the white elephant?"

"I heard about a white elephant in the Far East and made arrangements to purchase it from King Theebaw of Siam. When it arrived it was more gray than white.

169

However, Forepaugh was advertising that he had a true white elephant."

"And did he?"

"It was whitewashed," Barnum said.

"And you could prove that?"

"A news man from the *Philadelphia Press*, Alexander Kenealy, got close to the animal with a wet sponge."

"Did he print it?"

"No," Barnum said, "he brought the information to me and I let it be circulated."

"So that's why Forepaugh is threatening you?"

"That and other things," Barnum said. "The man is a thief. He says his elephant Bolivar is bigger than Jumbo; it isn't. He stole Dan Rice from me."

"Dan Rice?"

"A clown," Scott said.

"A clown."

"For the circus," Scott said.

"Ah."

"Threats started arriving in the post," Scott said. "They were against P. T. and Nancy."

"Forepaugh would not dare touch Nancy."

"He's not afraid of you, P. T.," Scott said. "You should have a bodyguard, and so should she."

"He's right, P. T.," Clint said. "It sounds like you both need protection."

"Would you do it?" Scott asked.

Clint looked at Scott, then back at P. T.

"Mr. Adams does not want to work for P. T. Barnum," Barnum said.

"I don't want to be put on *display*," Clint corrected.

"Then you'll take the job?" P. T. asked.

"I can recommend some good men—"

"You," Barnum said, "I want you, and you can bring anybody else along that you like. Price is no object."

Clint knew some people in New York who could use the work—if, indeed, they were still doing that kind of work.

"I can ask around," Clint said.

"But you can answer right now, can't you?" Scott asked.

"What brought you to New York, Clint?" Barnum asked, changing the subject.

"I come from time to time," Clint said.

"And why come to the circus?"

"Felicity wanted to go."

"And you told her you knew me?"

"I may have mentioned it."

Barnum slapped his hand down on his desk.

"You knew if you told her you knew me, she'd want to meet me," Barnum said, "and then you'd get to see me, as well."

"I don't think I put that much thought into going to the circus, P. T.," Clint replied.

"Nonsense," Barnum said, and then fell silent, as if the talking had tired him out.

"He has to rest," Scott said, standing up. "Mr. Adams, will you take on the job of protecting P. T. and Nancy?"

Clint looked at the old man behind the desk, whose head was now almost touching the desk top.

"Okay," Clint said, "okay, I'll do it."

Barnum lifted his head, winked, and said, "Welcome to the show business."

Nancy Barnum returned with Felicity just in time to take her husband upstairs and put him to bed. She exchanged words with Scott for a moment, then he accompanied Clint and Felicity to the front door.

"Nancy asked that you wait for her to come back down, if that's all right," Scott said, at the door.

"That's fine," Clint said.

"This is a beautiful house," Felicity said.

"P. T. designed it and had it built."

"I know," Felicity said, "Nancy was telling me." She looked at Clint. "She's very much in love with him. Did you know she met him when she was eight years old?"

"No, I didn't know that."

At that point, Nancy Barnum came down the stairs and approached Clint and Felicity.

"I just wanted to thank you for agreeing to help us," she said to Clint. "I'm so afraid that someone is going to try to hurt him."

"Or you," Scott said.

"That's not important," she said. "Phineas is the important one."

"Don't worry," Clint said, "I won't let anything happen to either of you."

"When will you be back?" she asked.

"I'll be back tomorrow," Clint said, "and I'll try to have a second man here then, also."

She took his hand and held it tightly.

"Thank you."

Embarrassed by her gratitude, he freed his hand and said, "Don't worry. I'll see you tomorrow."

"I'll be here tonight," Scott said, but Nancy ignored him.

"I have a buggy waiting outside to take you home," Scott said.

Clint and Felicity left the house and walked to the buggy.

"He's in love with her, you know," Felicity said.

Clint knew she was talking about Matthew Scott and said, "I know."

THIRTY-SIX

Clint wanted to use a man named Delvecchio to protect the Barnums. He was a private detective who lived in Brooklyn who Clint had met a couple of years ago when he was protecting a politician.

When they got back to the hotel, he sent Felicity off to her room and then went to talk to the desk clerk.

"I need someone to run an errand."

"What kind of errand?" the man asked.

"An expensive one."

"What does it entail?"

"A trip to Brooklyn."

"We have a bellhop who lives in Brooklyn."

"What's his name?"

"Harry."

"Is Harry working right now?"

"Yes, sir."

"I'll be in the bar. Could you have him come and see me?"

"Of course, sir."

"I may need him to be let off work for the rest of the evening. Can you arrange that?"

"I'll check with the manager?"

"With pay?"

The man smiled. "I'll check."

"All right, thanks."

Clint went into the bar, got himself a cold beer and took it with him to a corner table. A few moments later a bellhop appeared in the door. He looked around, and Clint waved once to call him over.

"Are you Mr. Adams?" he asked.

"That's right. Harry?"

"Yes, sir." He was a sad-faced man in his forties, with unusually large ears.

"Have a seat, Harry."

The bellhop looked around.

"I could get in trouble for sitting down with a guest."

"I'll take care of it."

Harry thought about it for a moment, then shrugged and sat down.

"I understand you live in Brooklyn."

"That's right."

"Do you know where Sackett Street is?"

"Yes, sir."

"Good," Clint said, "I'd like you to deliver a message to a man named Delvecchio."

"When?"

"Tonight."

"I gotta work."

"I'll get you off work with pay, plus *I'll* pay you to

deliver the message," Clint said. "What do you say?"

"You get me off work with pay," Harry said, "and I'm your man."

"Okay," Clint said, "let's go."

"Where?"

"To get me something to write with, and to talk to your boss."

THIRTY-SEVEN

The bellhop's name was Harry Cole, and the manager of the hotel was only too glad to make the man available to Clint Adams. He knew who Clint was and considered him an important guest.

When Harry was on his way to Brooklyn, Clint went up to his room and found Felicity waiting for him. This was, of course, no surprise, since she had spent the last few nights in his bed as well.

"What happened?" she asked as he undressed.

"I sent a message to a man I know," Clint said.

"A bodyguard?"

"A detective," Clint said, "but he'll be able to do the job."

"You're not angry with me, are you?"

He had sat down on the edge of the bed to remove his boots and turned to look at her over his shoulder.

179

"Why would I be angry with you?"

"Well, I'm the one who pushed you to see Barnum," she said. "Now, suddenly, you have a job, and you were here just to relax and get away."

This was true. Clint had spent the last few months looking rather hard for a horse to replace his beloved gelding, Duke, who'd had to be put out to pasture. He was starting to wonder if his days of riding the trail were over, because he just couldn't find a horse he wanted to keep for any period of time. Maybe it was time for him to be put out to pasture as well.

He'd come to New York to take some time off from horse hunting and had not expected to be pressed into service as a bodyguard for P. T. Barnum.

"If Barnum is truly in danger," Clint said, "I'm happy to help him. I just better not catch him trying to use this to make some money."

"Who's the man you sent the message to?"

"His name is Delvecchio."

"How will you know he got the message?"

"I'll find out tomorrow," he said, "one way or the other."

He finished undressing and got into bed with her naked. Beneath the sheet she was naked as well. He reached for her and drew her to him, enjoying the silky feel of her warm skin against his own. Her nipples were already hard and scraped his chest. He kissed her, sliding his hand down the line of her back, fitting his middle finger into the cleft between her buttocks. She scratched his back with her nails, then ran her hand down his back until she could scratch his butt as well.

"I'm sorry, anyway," she said, against his mouth.

"Why?"

"If you have to protect Barnum and his wife," she said, "we'll be seeing less of each other."

"That may be so," he said to her, "but not tonight."

In the morning, Clint slid from the bed without waking Felicity. He wanted to get an early start, but there was no reason she had to wake up. He slipped from the room quietly and went downstairs for breakfast. When he entered the Waldorf's dining room, he wasn't surprised to see Delvecchio sitting at a table, enjoying a huge breakfast.

"Good morning," he said, approaching the table.

Delvecchio looked up at him and smiled.

"I told them I was your guest," he said. "I hope you don't mind."

"I don't mind," Clint said. "Did you leave any food?"

"I think they'll be able to find something for you."

Clint sat down and the two men shook hands.

"Been a while," Delvecchio said. "I wondered if you'd get back to New York anytime soon."

"I'm back."

"And in trouble already?"

"Not trouble," Clint said. "Just a bit of work for you."

"What's the job?"

The waiter came over, and Clint ordered breakfast before telling Delvecchio what the job was.

"P. T. Barnum," Clint said.

"What about him?"

"What do you think of him?"

Delvecchio thought a moment, then said, "He could persuade Eskimos to pay to go and see ice."

"No other thoughts?"

Delvecchio shook his head and chewed his steak and eggs.

"The man has remarkably little impact on my life."

"Well, that could change."

"How?"

"He wants me to protect him and his wife," Clint said.

"And you're going to?"

"Not without help."

"Is he paying?"

"He is."

"Protect him against who?"

"A man named Forepaugh," Clint said, "or whoever else might be threatening him."

"Forepaugh?" Delvecchio asked. "Those two are fighting over white elephants or something. Does he really think Forepaugh would pay someone to hurt him?"

"Him or his wife."

"Bad business," Delvecchio said, "threatening a man's wife. Are you going to find out who it is?"

"Well, he did only want to hire us to protect them, not to find out who was making the threats."

"But finding the person making the threats would also be a way of protecting him."

"True. Is Eickhorst available?" He was referring to another man they had used in the past.

"He's out of town."

"Do you have someone else you can trust?"

"I can get someone," Delvecchio said. "When do you want to start?"

"Today."

"Where?"

Clint gave Delvecchio the address of Barnum's house on Astor Place.

"I'll be there this afternoon," Clint said. "Maybe Barnum or his wife can tell me something helpful. Or his young assistant."

"What about the assistant?" the detective asked. "Could he be involved somehow?"

"Maybe," Clint said. "It's my opinion that he's in love with Barnum's young wife."

"There's a motive."

"But he's also the one who brought me into it."

"Could be a cover-up," Delvecchio said, "but he'd be taking a big risk." Delvecchio chewed and swallowed. "Can you get Barnum to stay inside?"

"I doubt it."

"He's pretty old."

"And can't move very well, apparently."

Delvecchio made a face and said, "I guess I should take him, then. I'll put the other man on the wife."

"Who's the other man?"

"Not sure," Delvecchio said, "but I'll bring him by the house today for you to meet."

"Okay."

The waiter appeared with an impressive plate of steak and eggs and set it down in front of Clint.

"Can we get another basket of biscuits?" Delvecchio asked.

"Of course, sir."

"And butter," the man said, "lots of butter."

"Yes, sir."

As the waiter started away, Delvecchio called out, "Oh, could you bring some honey?"

The waiter turned and said, "Very good, sir."

"Listen," Clint said, cutting into his steak, "I want to thank you for coming on such short notice."

"Why not?" Delvecchio said, with a smile. "Working with you I meet such interesting people."

THIRTY-EIGHT

Matthew Scott answered the door when Clint knocked.

"Mr. Adams," he said. "Good morning."

"I think you should call me Clint, Matthew," Clint said. "After all, I'm going to be around for a while."

"All right, Clint. Come in."

"Is P. T. awake?" Clint asked after Scott closed the door.

"No," Scott said, "he's not an early riser at his age. In fact, he sleeps until quite late so that he will have the energy to go out at night to see the show."

"Does he attend every performance?"

"He tries."

"What about Mrs. Barnum? Nancy? Is she awake?"

"Yes," Scott said. "I was just about to leave to go to the Garden and make sure everything was all right for the show tonight. I'll get her for you and then be off."

"Fine," Clint said.

"Uh, why do you want her, exactly?"

"We need to talk," Clint said, "if I'm going to be going in and out of here."

"About what?"

"Things, Matthew," Clint said, "things. I'll need to know her routine, and P. T.'s, that sort of thing."

"Oh, well, okay. I'll get her."

He left to go into the bowels of the house and, when he returned, Nancy Barnum was with him.

"I'm so happy to see you, Mr. Adams," she said. "I feel safer already."

"Nancy, I have to go to the Garden, but I'll be back soon," Scott said.

"That's all right, Matt," she said. "Mr. Adams is here now."

"Uh, yes," Scott said, "all right. Well, I'll see you both later."

Clint nodded and Scott went out the door.

"Can we talk somewhere, Nancy?"

"Of course," she said. "Come in the living room."

He followed her and they sat on the sofa, with one full cushion between them.

"I'm bringing in two men to help me with this job," Clint said.

"Two men?"

"One to stay with you, and one to stay with P. T."

"You're not staying?"

"Nancy, I think the best way for me to protect you and P. T. is to find out who's been threatening you, and if they really mean it."

"Phineas thinks it's Adam Forepaugh."

"What do you think?"

"Me? I'm sure I don't know."

"Nancy, has anything more serious than a threat taken place?"

"You mean, have there been any attempts to hurt P. T.?"

"Or you."

"No," she said, "nothing like that has happened so far, thank God."

"How well do you know Matthew?"

"Matt? He's worked for P. T. for several years."

"Did you know him before that?"

"No," she said, "Phineas met him first."

"What do you think of him?"

"I think he's very good at his job."

"Nothing else?"

"What else could there be."

"Well . . . forgive me, but you are a young woman, and P. T. is considerably older—"

"Stop," she said, closing her eyes. "I won't hear that kind of talk. I love my husband, Mr. Adams. I would not take up with another man for any reason."

"Not even with one who loved you?"

"Loved—what are you saying?"

"It's my opinion that Matthew Scott is in love with you."

"In love with me? Why, that's ridiculous."

"Is it? You're a lovely young woman, Nancy, and he's a young man. He's around you all the time. Don't you think it possible he could have fallen in love with you somewhere along the way?"

"I don't—but I've *never* given him any indication— I never would."

"I know that," Clint said. "Believe me, I'm not accusing you of anything, but if I'm going to get to the bottom of this, and protect both of you, I need to know all of the details."

"There has never been anything between Matthew Scott and me."

"I believe you . . . but do you trust him?"

"I . . . Phineas trusts him."

"But do you?"

"Are you saying that maybe Matthew has something to do with the threats?" she asked.

"I'm trying to eliminate him in my mind," Clint said. "Could Matthew have been bought off by Forepaugh?"

She paused a moment, then said, "I suppose anything is possible."

"But you don't believe it?"

"No," she said, "I believe Matthew to be loyal to Phineas."

"All right, then," Clint said. "Let's go on to something else, now."

"To what?"

"Tell me something about the everyday occurrences in this house, and in your and P. T.'s lives . . ."

THIRTY-NINE

After they had discussed the comings and goings during the course of the day in the house, complete with the duties of the servants, Nancy walked Clint through the house, showing him all the entrances and "egresses." After a few hours spent together, Clint was convinced of two things. One, he knew all he needed to know about the house. Two, it would be very easy for a young man like Matthew Scott to fall in love with Nancy Barnum.

They were returning to the living room when there was a knock at the front door.

"Matthew?" he asked, looking at her.

"No," she said, "Matthew has a key."

Ah, so he *didn't* know everything there was to know about the house. He'd have to ask her who else had a key.

"I'll get it."

189

He went to the door and opened it. On the doorstep were Delvecchio and a young woman.

"Hello, Clint," the detective said, "meet my friend, Sam."

"Sam?"

"Samantha," the girl said. "I'm very glad to meet you, Mr. Adams."

"Likewise," Clint said. They shook hands, and he found that she had a firm grip. She was medium height, blonde, and built quite well. In fact, the clothing she was wearing did little to hide the fact that she had a very impressive physique. She was wearing jeans that fit her quite well, and a man's shirt that did little to hide the thrust of her full breasts. Her hair was very pale blond, as were her eyebrows, which made them almost invisible.

"You're staring," Delvecchio said.

"Oh, I'm sorry," Clint said, addressing Samantha, "but I was expecting another man."

"I thought Mrs. Barnum might be more comfortable with a woman around," Delvecchio said.

"Is that a problem?" Sam asked Clint. "I assure you I'm very good at my job. I have some background with the police department—three years, in fact."

"And then what happened?"

"I quit."

"May I ask why?"

"I didn't like the jobs they were giving me."

"What was wrong with them?"

"They were for girls."

"And this one isn't?"

"The fact that I'll be protecting a woman," Sam said, "does not make this a woman's job."

"Good point, Sam," Clint said. "Why don't you both come in? I've kept you on the doorstep long enough."

"Thank you," she said.

Sam went in first and as Delvecchio passed Clint, the detective met Clint's puzzled glance with an amused one of his own.

Clint closed the door and turned to face the duo.

"Why don't we go into the living room and I'll introduce you to Mrs. Barnum," he said.

He led the way and made the introductions. Nancy was told she should simply call them "Delvecchio" and "Sam."

"No first name, Mr. Delvecchio?" she asked.

He smiled and said, "Not one I'd like to divulge, Mrs. Barnum."

"And no last name for you?" she asked Sam.

"Sharpe," Sam said, "but I don't use it much. I just answer to Sam."

Clint could see that the two women were the same age. They were both attractive in different ways, and he hoped they would be able to get along. If they didn't, he was going to have to find someone else for the job.

"Well," Nancy said, "you'll both just have to call me Nancy. Can I get anyone a drink? Some coffee? Tea?"

"I'd love a cup of tea," Sam said. "Why don't I come with you to get it?"

The two women left, and Delvecchio said, "That'll give them a chance to get to know each other a little bit. You want to show me around the house?"

Clint gave Delvecchio the same tour Nancy had given him. During the tour the detective said, "Where's Barnum."

"Apparently, he's still in bed."

"Does he always sleep this late?"

"So I've been told."

"Then he goes to the show?"

"Yes."

"Gonna be real hard to protect him there."

"I know. I was there last night. They draw quite a crowd, but they take him in and out a special entrance."

"I'll need to meet his driver."

"Good point," Clint said. "I'll introduce you to Matthew Scott when he gets back, and he can introduce you to the driver."

"What about this Scott?" Delvecchio asked. "Did you talk to Mrs. Barnum about him?"

"I did," Clint said. "She seems to think he's completely loyal to her husband."

"And in love with her?"

"She says no."

"She doesn't see it."

"Not at all."

"That's not surprising. Maybe she just doesn't want to see it."

"You could be right."

"Tell me something," Clint said.

"What?"

"You and Sam."

"What do you want to know?"

"Are you a couple?"

"Why, are you interested?"

"That's not why I asked," Clint said. "I want to know what the emotional consequences could be to having the two of you work together."

"Well, that's all we do," Delvecchio said, "we work

together. There's nothing emotional going on besides friendship. Okay?"

"Okay."

After they finished the tour, they returned to the living room and found Nancy and Sam having their tea and laughing about something.

"Oh, there you two are," Sam said.

"What are you laughing about?"

"Men."

"We're funny?" Clint asked.

"As a group, yes," Sam said. "Individually . . . well, that depends on the man, I guess."

Nancy stood up and said, "I have to go up and wake Phineas and start to get him ready."

"The show isn't for hours," Clint said.

"It takes him a while to wake up."

"Let me come with you," Delvecchio said. "I need to know what goes on around here."

"All right," she said, "but he probably won't notice you right away, or remember that you met until later."

"That's all right," Delvecchio said. "I just want to get an idea of what happens."

Nancy looked at Clint.

"Will you still be here?"

"I'd like to talk to you some more, Nancy," he said, "but maybe later, all right? I'm going to go down to Madison Square Garden and take a look around. I can let myself out."

"All right, then," she said. "I'll see you later. Sam?"

"I'll be here, Nancy."

Nancy nodded and then led Delvecchio from the room.

"We're not sleeping together," Sam said to Clint.

"What?"

"Delvecchio and me," she said. "We don't sleep together."

"So he told me."

"We just work together."

"He told me that, too."

"Why don't I let you out and make sure the door locks behind you?" she suggested.

"All right."

They walked to the front door and before he left she said to him, "Don't worry, I won't let anything happen to her."

"I believe you," he said, "but I think I'll worry anyway. It'll keep me on my toes."

"Suit yourself," she said, and closed the door on him. He stood there a moment and only left when he heard the lock.

FORTY

When Clint reached Madison Square Garden, it wasn't anywhere nearly as crowded as it had been the night before. He encountered a security guard at the front entrance, but Scott had apparently given his name out and the man allowed him to pass.

"Would you know where Mr. Scott is?"

"No, sir," the man said, "no idea."

"Have you let anyone else pass today?"

"Just whoever's on the list."

"How many before me?"

"Two."

"Both men?"

"Yes."

"What was their business?"

"That's not for me to know, sir," the man said. "If their name is on the list, I let them pass. I assume that their business is with Mr. Scott or Mr. Barnum."

"All right," Clint said. "Thanks."

Clint entered the huge structure and wondered where to look for Scott first. He decided on two places, either the office, or the Garden floor, where the show always took place.

It took some walking around to find his way to the office, and then when he tried the door, it was locked. He knocked, but there was no answer. He listened at the door, but it didn't sound like anyone was inside. He turned and started trying to find his way to the Garden's floor.

In the center of the floor, Jumbo was being put through his motions by his handler. Off to the side, two men were talking.

"What do you mean he's hired a new bodyguard?" one man asked. "Who, for Chrissake?"

"A man named Clint Adams," the second man said.

"I know that name," the first man said. "Christ, they've written books about him, haven't they?"

"Just some dime novels," the second man said. "You can't believe everything you read in dime novels."

"Well, if only half of it is true, then I'm gonna be needing some help."

"Then get some," the second man said. "The way I hear it, Adams is bringing in some help, too."

"You know," the first man said. "This was supposed to be an easy job. Take care of some old man."

"You thought it was going to be easy?" the first man asked. "I never did."

"Yeah, well, you're right again," the first one said.

"You love bein' right. That should make you real happy."

"Actually," the second man said, "it kind of does."

Clint found his way because he heard Jumbo doing whatever it is elephants do—trumpeting? Whatever it was, it was a loud sound and he was able to follow it. When he saw Jumbo, it was from a considerably closer vantage point than he had seen the animal the night before. He was shocked at the sheer size of him and wondered if Adam Forepaugh could really have a creature that was larger.

There was one man working with Jumbo, and nobody else was on the floor. Clint moved out farther so he could look up into the seats. He thought he saw someone, but if they had been there, they were gone.

"Hey!"

He turned and saw Jumbo's handler.

"You're not supposed to be here."

"I have clearance—" Clint started, but the man cut him off.

"I don't care what you got," the man said. "Don't come any closer to this elephant. Understand?"

"Don't worry," Clint said, putting his hands up, and his palms out at shoulder level, "I don't intend to. Have you seen Matthew Scott?"

"Yeah," the man said, "a few minutes ago, but he ain't around now."

"Do you know where he went?"

"No. Try the office."

"I tried that."

"Well, try again," the man said. "You came in that way, and he went out that way." He pointed to an entrance across from the one Clint had used to come in. "He can get to the office from there."

"Okay," Clint said, "I'll try again. Thanks."

But the man was no longer paying him any attention. He was talking to the elephant. Clint turned, went back out the way he had come and retraced his steps to the office.

After Clint left, the two men came out from the alcove they had ducked behind.

"We've got to be more careful," the second one said. "We can't afford to be seen together."

"That's fine with me," the first one said. "The next time I want to see you is when I get paid."

"Do the job and you will be."

"Don't worry," the first man said, "it'll get done."

FORTY-ONE

When Clint got back to the office, he tried the door again but still found it locked. However, this time it sounded like someone was inside. He heard what sounded like drawers opening and closing. He knocked and waited. There were footsteps, and then the door opened.

"There you are," he said to Matthew Scott. "I've been looking for you."

"Come on in," Scott said, walking back into the room and leaving the door open. "I was down on the floor for a while and just got back."

Clint entered, saw the desk with the drawers open.

"Looking for something?"

"Yes, I am," Scott said moving around behind the desk again. He started closing the drawers. "I'm looking for some papers that P. T. seems to have forgotten where he put."

"Does he do that a lot?" Clint asked. "Forget?"

Scott looked sad and said, "More and more, lately." He stood there behind the desk, looking around the room, as if trying to figure out where to look next.

"Can we talk?" Clint asked.

"Why not?" Scott said. "I can't find what I'm looking for. What do you want to talk about?"

"Threats," Clint said, "and who might have motive to make them, other than Forepaugh. Also, I'd like to know where I can find Forepaugh."

Scott looked directly at Clint.

"I thought you were going to protect P. T.?"

"I am."

"Then why do you want to find Forepaugh?"

"The way I can best protect P. T. and Nancy is to find out who's making the threats and why, and to put a stop to it before it goes beyond threats."

"And how are you going to do that," Scott asked, "and keep them safe at the same time?"

"There are already two people at P. T.'s house to watch over both he and Nancy," Clint said. "A man named Delvecchio and a woman named Samantha Sharpe. You'll meet them both when you get back there."

"A woman?"

"I think Nancy would be more comfortable with a woman around her, don't you?" Clint asked.

"You're probably right."

Clint didn't bother telling Scott that this was not his idea. He'd apologize later to Delvecchio for taking the credit.

"All right," Scott said, "I'll give you Forepaugh's address. He lives up near the park."

Central Park. Clint had been there before.

"And who else would want to threaten P. T.?" Clint asked. "Or harm him?"

"Lots of people would," Scott said. "He is not as beloved as he thinks, or as most people think. He has competitors, enemies, more of them than just Adam Forepaugh."

"I'll need their names and addresses as well."

Scott looked down at the desk and said, "I'll sit right here and write them out for you."

"Then what are you going to do?"

"I suppose I'll go back to the house and see if I can find what I'm looking for there."

"Do you live at the house, Matthew?"

"At the Barnum house? No, I have my own place. It's just a couple of rooms, really, but quite comfortable."

"I see."

"What made you ask if I lived at the house?"

"I was just wondering," Clint said. "You were there early today."

"I get there early every day."

"We're going to need your schedule, then," Clint said. "You better write that down as well."

"All right," Scott said, seating himself. "And what are you planning for the rest of the day?"

"Well, I suppose I'll go back to the house and introduce you to my two people," Clint said, "and then I may have a talk with the police."

"Why the police?"

"To find out why they're not taking the threats to P. T. more seriously."

"Good luck," Scott said. "I talked to them until I was blue in the face. Lieutenant Egan just wouldn't listen—"

"*Lieutenant* Egan?" Clint asked.

"You know him?"

"I did, a couple of years ago," Clint said, "but he was a sergeant then, and not the world's most reliable policeman."

"Then he hasn't changed all that much, except for rank," Scott said.

"I guess I'll just have to find that out for myself."

FORTY-TWO

Clint tucked in his pocket the list Scott made and then went back to the Barnum house with the young man. After introducing him to Delvecchio and Samantha Sharpe, he went down to the police station on Centre Street to see if he could find Lieutenant Egan. He'd met Egan during the same trip to New York when he had met Teddy Roosevelt. He'd been very impressed with Roosevelt, but not impressed with Egan at all. The man had his own agenda and was not above running errands for wealthy, self-involved politicians.

When he asked for "Lieutenant" Egan at Centre Street, he was told to sit down and wait. No one took his name, so when Egan appeared and saw him he reacted with surprise.

Egan's appearance had deteriorated in two years, even if his position at the police department had improved.

He was a shambling, disheveled man. The only things that hadn't changed were his ham-sized hands.

"Well, well," Egan said, "as I live and breathe, the great Clint Adams is back in New York. What brings you back to the big city, Adams?"

"Well," Clint said, "I was here to take in the circus, but now it seems I've gotten involved in something else."

"And that would be?"

Clint stood up, because he didn't like having Egan glowering down at him.

"P. T. Barnum."

Egan squinted.

"What about him?"

"Somebody's threatening him, and the police aren't doing anything about it," Clint said.

"What's your interest?"

"He's a friend of mine."

"You got high and mighty friends, ain'tcha?" Egan asked.

"Don't hate me because I attract a better brand of friends that you, lieutenant," Clint said. "When did you make lieutenant, anyway?"

"Not long after you left last time."

"On your way to captain?"

"You never know."

"Must be a heavily favor-laden road you travel, Egan."

The policeman frowned and asked, "What does that mean?"

"Nothing," Clint said. "What about Barnum?"

"He says he's being threatened," Egan said. "We don't see it that way."

"Why not?"

"Because we ain't seen any of the notes or letters he claims he received." Egan smiled. "Have you?"

"No," Clint said, "not yet."

"And you won't," Egan said. "You might be ready to take his word for it, Adams, but the police ain't."

"Why not?"

"Because, in my opinion, it's just another P. T. Barnum humbug attempt to get some publicity," Egan said. "After all, the old boy is slipping, you know. He's afraid the public will forget him."

"I don't think that would ever happen."

"Maybe not," Egan said, "but he does."

"So you're not going to take any action?"

"Not unless somebody can prove to me he's being threatened," Egan said, "or unless something happens."

"Like somebody kills him?"

"Why would somebody want to kill him?" Egan asked. "The old boy's got one foot in the grave already."

"Egan," Clint said, "I can really see why they promoted you to lieutenant."

Egan stuck his jaw out and said, "Don't get in my way this time around, Adams. I told you last time we'd tangle and we didn't—lucky for you. You might not be so lucky this time."

"I guess we'll just have to wait and see who gets lucky," Clint said, "and who doesn't."

He left Egan there with his jaw jutting out pugnaciously.

FORTY-THREE

"Phineas threw them away," Nancy said.

"What?" Clint asked. "Why?"

"He said he didn't want them in the house. He said he didn't want me to see them."

"Wait a minute." Clint looked at Nancy, then at Matthew Scott. Behind them, involved only as observers, were Delvecchio and Sam. "You never saw these threatening letters?"

"No," she said.

"Did you?" he asked Scott.

"No."

"Then how do we know they existed?"

"Phineas told me they existed," Nancy said, firming her jaw.

"Suppose this is one of his publicity stunts?"

"I believe him," Nancy said.

"Scott?"

"Sorry, Clint," Scott said. "I believe him, too."

Clint was going to have to isolate Scott away from Nancy. He was in love with her and would not contradict her—not in her presence, anyway.

"I want to talk to P. T.," Clint said.

"He's in his office," Nancy said. "I'll take you there."

He looked at Delvecchio and Sam.

"Have you met him yet?"

"Yes," Delvecchio said.

"All right," Clint said. "I'll talk to him alone then."

Delvecchio shrugged, and Sam looked unaffected. After all, her focus was on Nancy, not P. T.

Nancy led Clint to P. T.'s office but stopped just outside and turned to face him.

"I thought you were his friend." Her tone was accusing, as was the look on her face.

"Nancy," Clint said, "are you going to tell me that P. T. Barnum is above pulling a publicity stunt for attention?"

"In the past, no," she said. "But not this time."

"So you're telling me he's changed?"

"No," she said, "he hasn't changed at all. He's still the brilliant showman he always was. All I'm saying is that *this* time it's not a stunt."

"Well," Clint said, "I hope you're right."

"I am," she said. "You'll see."

She opened the office door and said, "P. T., Clint is here to see you."

"Come in, come in, my boy!" Barnum's greeting was magnanimous and energetic. He looked quite different from the man Clint had seen the night before, being helped from the room by Nancy.

"I'll leave you two alone," she said. "Clint, will you be staying for dinner?"

"No, thank you, Nancy," he said.

"I'll tell the cook, then, to set places for Delvecchio and Sam, only."

She withdrew and closed the door behind her.

"She's something, isn't she?" Barnum asked. "What she ever saw in a broken down old wreck like me I'll never know—but I'll be eternally grateful."

"P. T., we have to talk."

"Well, have a seat, lad," Barnum said. "Let's talk. You look very serious."

Clint sat down across from the man, who looked completely rested. He wondered how long these spurts of energy lasted.

"It's about these threats against you."

"What about them?"

"The police tell me there's no proof," Clint said. "They haven't seen the letters and notes. Nancy also says she hasn't seen them. Neither has Scott."

"I see where this is going," Barnum said. "You think the 'Master of Humbug' has struck again, eh?"

"I think it's very possible, yes," Clint said.

"I don't blame you, my boy," Barnum said. "In your place I'd think the same thing."

"Nancy's very upset with me."

Barnum waved that off.

"She's very protective of me," he said. "She'll get over it, I assure you. The question we must deal with now is, how can I convince you I'm telling the truth?"

"There's only one way, I'm afraid."

"And what's that?"

"Show me a note."

"You won't take my word for it?"

Clint measured his words before speaking.

"Don't take offense, P. T.," he said, "but if I'm going to invest a block of my time in protecting you, I need to be sure you need protection."

"Well, we're at an impasse, then," Barnum said, "because I have none of the notes. I could fake one, but that wouldn't accomplish anything. I can only promise you one thing."

"And what's that?"

"As soon as I get another one," Barnum said, "I'll hand it right over to you."

Clint stared at the man.

"Is that good enough?"

"I guess it's going to have to be," Clint said, "isn't it?"

"For now, I guess," Barnum agreed.

"P. T.," Clint said, "if I find out this has all been one of your hoaxes—"

"The benefit of the doubt, Clint," Barnum said, interrupting him, "that's all I ask of you."

"And that's all I'm going to give you right now."

FORTY-FOUR

Delvecchio caught Clint in the foyer of the house, alone, and put the question to him.

"So what's the verdict?" he asked. "Is he in danger or isn't he?"

"I'm giving him the benefit of the doubt right now," Clint said. "He'll show us the next note he gets—if he gets another one."

"But who's to say he won't have written it?" the detective asked.

Clint scratched the corner of his mouth to keep it from twitching.

"You know," he said, "I met P. T. years ago and refused to be sucked into his world. Where did I go wrong here?"

"I don't know," Delvecchio said, "but knowing you, I'll bet a woman is involved."

"You're right."

"Somebody you're serious about?"

"No," Clint said. "Somebody I met a few days ago, and I guess I just saw this as a chance to impress her."

"The only reason I ask if it's serious," Delvecchio said, "is that Sam asked me about you."

"You mean . . . you two really aren't sleeping together?"

"Nope," Delvecchio said. "Never have, never will."

"Why not?"

"Because, we're friends," he said, "and we want to stay that way."

"Oh."

"Don't you have any women friends, Clint?"

"Well, sure—"

"That you haven't slept with?"

Clint frowned.

"I'm sure there are some," he answered, "but I'm a little busy right now to be able to think of them."

"That's okay," Delvecchio said. "You don't have to name them. What's your next move going to be?"

"I think," Clint said, "that I'll have a talk with P. T.'s competition—Mr. Adam Forepaugh."

"Tonight?"

"No," Clint said, "in the morning."

"Will you be at the show tonight, then?"

"I thought I'd show up and watch the crowd."

"And bring your lady friend?"

"Not while we're working," he said. "She knows that."

"I wonder if she knows," Delvecchio said, "that you'll be working with Samantha."

"Now Delvecchio," Clint said, "why start trouble?"

FORTY-FIVE

Clint went back to the hotel and had dinner with Felicity Parker, who told him she was leaving New York in the morning.

"Why?"

"Because," she said, "I don't think it's going to get any better than it's been. You're busy now, and I have to get back to my life. Do you know what my life is?"

Guiltily, he said, "No."

"And you don't need to know," she said. "These past few days have been wonderful, but it's time for me to go."

"All right."

She reached out and put her hand on his.

"I knew you wouldn't be too disappointed." It was the most mature thing he had heard her say.

"Felicity—"

"No," she said, "it's all right. I want you to stay here now. I'm going to go to my room and sleep there, and in the morning I will check out and go home."

She stood up, came around to his side of the table and kissed him.

"Thank you for a wonderful time."

"You're welcome."

She left the dining room, and he never saw her again.

In the morning he rose and realized that the maids had changed his bed the day before, and he could not smell Felicity on his sheets. That suited him. She was out of his life now, and he was out of hers. They were both going on with their own lives.

He went downstairs and had breakfast, and then got a cab in front of the hotel and gave the driver the address he had for Adam Forepaugh. He did not know if the man had an office, or if he would be home. He would find out when he got there.

The cab let him off in front of a two-story home built of brick and concrete. He had to go up seven stone steps to reach the front door. There was a huge, ornate brass knocker on the door and he used it. The door was answered by a tall, cadaverously thin man with pale skin except for dark circles beneath his eyes. His thinning grey hair came to a pronounced widow's peak. He could have been fifty or seventy or anywhere in between.

"Yes?"

"I'd like to see Mr. Forepaugh."

"For what reason?"

"It's a private matter."

"Mr. Forepaugh does not see people on private matters."

"It concerns P. T. Barnum."

The man's eyes flickered just once, but it was enough to indicate interest.

"What is your name?"

"Clint Adams."

"Wait here, please."

He closed the door gently in Clint's face. Clint began to count. When he reached one hundred and ninety-nine the door opened again and the man said, "Please come this way."

This home was not as ostentatious as P. T. Barnum's, but it had taken a lot of money to build and furnish it, nevertheless. He followed the butler—or whatever he was—to a pair of double doors, which the man swung open to reveal a room filled with bookshelves and a man seated behind a desk. There had been books in Barnum's office, but every inch of wall space in this room was covered with books.

"Come in, sir," the man behind the desk said. "I am Adam Forepaugh."

Forepaugh was younger than Barnum, older than Clint. He appeared to be somewhere in his late fifties, perhaps even his early sixties.

"Thank you for seeing me."

"That will be all, Bennett. Close the doors."

"Yes, sir."

"Please," Forepaugh said, "have a seat."

Clint sat in a very comfortable chair, directly across from Forepaugh.

"I know you think that mentioning Barnum's name got you in here," the man said, "but you are wrong. It was the mention of your own name that gained you entry."

"Really?"

"You see, I know who you are, I know your reputation. I am prepared to make you a very generous offer—"

"I'm already working for P. T. Barnum, Mr. Forepaugh."

The man behind the desk waved that off and said, "I'll pay you double what he's paying you."

"You don't even know what I'm doing for him."

"I know what I'll have you doing for me, sir."

"Mr. Forepaugh," Clint said, shaking his head, "I am not working for P. T. Barnum as a performer."

"Then he's a fool."

"I've been hired to protect him."

That stopped Forepaugh for about a minute.

"Protect Phineas?" he asked. "From what? Who?"

"Well," Clint said, "he seems to think it's from you."

Forepaugh sat back.

"Are you here to kill me, then?"

"Not at all," Clint said.

"Then why are you here, sir?"

"To find out if you are threatening P. T. Barnum and his wife."

Forepaugh studied Clint for a few moments, and then relaxed a bit. Apparently, he was satisfied that Clint was not there to kill him.

"I might threaten P. T.," he said, then, "if I thought it would do any good, but why would I threaten Nancy? P. T. knows better than that."

"Does he?"

"He should!" Forepaugh said. "But wait—are you sure he's being threatened?"

Clint didn't answer.

"You're not, are you?"

He still didn't answer.

"This could be a publicity stunt on his part, and you have been sucked into it," Forepaugh said.

"That remains to be seen," Clint finally said.

"Ah ha!" Forepaugh said. "I knew it. You are not even sure yourself. I suspect you'll be very angry if it does turn out to be one more big humbug on his part. He wants one, you know."

"One what?"

"One more big triumph before he dies."

"Doesn't everyone?"

"Not the way P. T. does."

"What's this I hear about white elephants?"

"Bah!" Forepaugh said. "That's business. My white elephant is outdrawing his because his isn't really white—but that is business, I say. I wouldn't threaten P. T. over business."

"You wouldn't?"

"Of course not," Forepaugh said. "If not for P. T., I wouldn't be in the show business. He paved the way. I have tremendous respect and admiration for him, and he knows it."

"Why would he suspect you, then?"

"He wouldn't," Forepaugh said. "That's what makes me think it's one big ruse on his part."

"Do you know anyone who would threaten him, if not you?"

"Tons of people," Forepaugh said. "They'd threaten me and P. T. In fact, if I were him, I'd watch out for that young Matthew Scott."

"Why Scott?"

"Because the young pup is after P. T.'s wife," Forepaugh said. "Any fool can see he's in love with her."

Clint considered that for a moment.

"But I see you've already thought of that."

"Yes."

"Did you talk to Nancy about it?"

"Yes."

"And?"

"She thinks it's ridiculous."

"She's a sweet girl," Forepaugh said. "I don't know how the old fool got her, but he doesn't deserve her. She'd never think that Scott would be disloyal to P. T."

"And you think he would be?"

"For the right amount of money, anyone would be disloyal."

"I'm not sure I believe that."

"Which means you are a man without a price?"

Clint didn't respond.

"Or a man whose price has simply not been reached yet?"

"The first, I hope."

"That would be nice," Forepaugh said, "to find a man with integrity. I'm afraid there's a terrible lack of them in the show business."

"Except for you?"

"And Phineas."

"You think P. T. has integrity?"

"He gives people what he says he will give them," Forepaugh said. "He gives them what he wants. Sometimes it involves slight of hand, but no one is ever hurt by it. No, there is no lack of integrity in P. T."

Clint had to admit, Forepaugh sounded as if he actually admired the older showman.

"I'm ruining your image of me, aren't I?" Forepaugh asked.

"I'm afraid so."

"Look," Forepaugh said, "put your mind at rest. I am not threatening P. T. I hope the old goat goes on for ten or twenty more years. The competition is good for both of us. Look elsewhere for your culprit, Mr. Adams. He is not sitting before you."

"I'll keep that in mind, Mr. Forepaugh," Clint said, standing. "Thank you for seeing me."

"And please," Forepaugh said, "think about my offer. I would pay you highly as a performer."

"I'm afraid performing on stage is not in my future, Mr. Forepaugh," Clint said, "but I do thank you for the offer. I can find my own way out, thanks."

FORTY-SIX

Clint could have gone back to the Barnum house but decided he didn't want to see any of the people who were there right now. Instead, he went back to his hotel to do some thinking over a cold beer.

Forepaugh had been very convincing. On the other hand, so had Barnum. If he believed both of them, then it became obvious that someone else was sending threats to Barnum. He took out the piece of paper he'd gotten from Matthew Scott. On it were four names, the people Scott thought might have reason to threaten or harm P. T. Barnum and his wife.

First was a man named Jack Seward, who had been recently fired as Jumbo's handler for being drunk. He said he'd get Barnum.

There was also Otto Fleckstein, who had been arrested for skimming from the nightly take of the show. He had been released on bail and a trial was pending. Barnum was set to testify against him.

Third was a fellow named Harvey Wetlock, who claimed that Barnum had broken up his relationship with a woman named Edna Calhoun. Edna worked for Barnum's show, and Barnum had convinced her that Wetlock was not the man for her.

The last name on the list was a surprise to Clint, because he had not looked at the list as soon as he had been handed it. The name was Lieutenant Gerald Egan of the New York City Police Department. Apparently, Barnum had caused the man "embarrassment" on more than one occasion, and he had threatened to "get" Barnum. He made at least one such threat right in front of Matthew Scott.

And what about Matthew Scott? Clint had to trust the man completely in order to believe this list he had made. He was going to have to speak to the four men on the list, get some idea of whether or not these things were true and then pass his own judgment on Scott. If he believed him, then he could take some action against the men on the list. If, however, he did not believe him, then he had to disregard the list and concentrate on Scott.

He folded the list and put it away. The first order of business, then, was to determine Matthew Scott's reliability.

He left his beer half finished and left for Madison Square Garden to attend the show.

He was able to gain entry into the Garden easily enough. After walking through the halls, following the sounds of the show, he found Sam standing with Nancy in one of the entry halls.

"Where's P. T.?" he asked.

"He's in his box," Nancy said. "That's where he watches the show from each night."

"And why are you out here?" Clint asked. "Don't you usually watch it with him from the box?"

"I did," Nancy said, "but Sam would not let me go up there."

Clint looked at Sam.

"It's better to keep the two targets apart," she said, "at least while they're in public."

"Good point. Where's Delvecchio?"

"Del's in the box with P. T."

"And where's Matthew Scott?"

Sam and Nancy exchanged a glance, then Nancy said, "We don't know."

"Where does he usually watch the show from?"

"He moves around to watch it from all angles, looking for something wrong," Nancy said. "It's something P. T. used to do. He always said he had to see the show from the same vantage point as the crowd."

"All right," Clint said. "Which way does P. T. come after the show?"

"This way," Nancy said. "That's why we're waiting here."

"And then what?"

"It's a short walk from here to the office. From there we hustle him out a private exit and into a cab, and we take him home."

"What does he do when he gets home?"

"He has a cup of tea, goes over the performance in his mind and waits to hear what the night's take was."

"And nobody's ever tried anything while he's been in his box?"

"Some people try to reach him to shake his hand or to touch him," Nancy said. "But that's all."

"Is anyone else in the box with him?"

"Two security men. They bring him down when the show's almost over."

"And how soon will that be, now?"

"About an hour."

"Okay," Clint said. "You ladies stay here, then."

"What are you going to do?" Sam asked.

"I'm going to take a page from P. T.'s book," he said. "He likes to see what his customers see, that's what I'm going to do. I'm going to move around and see how they see *him*."

"Good idea," Sam said.

Clint excused himself and went off to make a circuit of the Garden floor.

Two men were in the stands directly across from P. T. Barnum's box.

"Who's that with him?" the second man asked.

"I don't know."

"I thought Clint Adams was protecting him."

"He is."

"Then that man works for Adams?"

"I suppose."

"I'm leaving," the second man said. "When you get all the facts—like who *that* man is—you let me know. Until then, I don't make a move."

The first man started to protest, but in the end he just let the second man go and resumed staring across the Garden at P. T. Barnum, the man he hated.

FORTY-SEVEN

Clint found six different viewpoints of Barnum from which he could have shot him. If someone wanted the old showman dead, he would have been dead by now. If threats were being made, something else was being planned than just killing him.

He made his way back to where Sam and Nancy were standing, waiting for P. T. to be brought down by the security guards and Delvecchio.

"Any minute now," Nancy said.

"Did you see anything suspicious?" Sam asked.

"No," he said, so only she could hear him, "but I could have taken a clean shot half a dozen times. Something else is going on here."

"You mean somebody doesn't want to kill him?"

"Not outright," Clint said, "or they could have done it by now."

"Maybe they want to drag it out," she said, "make him wait for it. Make him worry."

"Well," Clint said, "he doesn't seem to be worried."

"You think he's lying?"

"P. T. would never call it a lie," Clint said. "He'd say he was creating an atmosphere for something."

"Which means we're wasting our time?"

"Not while you're getting paid, you're not."

"Look," she said, "I'd rather be working for somebody who really needs me. It's not the money."

"Sorry," he said, "no offense."

"None taken."

There was a roar from the crowd, and Clint was wondering if the finale had started.

"I talked to Adam Forepaugh today. Did Del fill you in on him?"

"The competition? Yeah. What'd you find out from him?"

"I don't think he's the one sending the threats," Clint said.

"What makes you say that?"

"He sounds as though he really respects P. T. and values their competition. He feels they'd both lose out if they weren't competing."

"So if not him, then who?"

"I have a few names," he said, "but first I need to check out the man who gave me the names."

"Scott?"

"Yeah."

"He's so in love with Nancy," she said, lowering her voice.

"I know."

"And she doesn't see it."

"Or refuses to."

She looked him in the eye and said, "I can always tell when a man likes me."

"Yes," he said, returning her look, "but can you tell when he loves you?"

"I don't know," she admitted. "I've never had a man love me before."

Before Clint could reply, the security guards and Delvecchio showed up with Barnum. The two guards were burly, and were practically carrying him.

"Phineas?" Nancy said.

"I'm fine."

Delvecchio nodded at Clint and said aloud to everyone, "Let's get him out of here."

"Go, go," Clint said. "Sam, take Nancy."

They all went into the hall and down to the office. Clint thought Barnum looked comical being hurried along the way he did. Once or twice he saw the man's legs work, but his feet were not touching the floor.

They went through the office and out a private entrance. There they found Barnum's buggy and driver waiting. There was room for Barnum, Nancy, Delvecchio and Sam.

"What about you?" Sam asked.

"I'll be along later," Clint said.

"It was a marvelous show tonight," Barnum said to Nancy, as if he didn't notice anyone else.

"Yes, dear."

"Did you see any of it?"

"Yes, I did."

Clint looked at the driver and said, "Go!"

The driver snapped his reins, and the horse started forward. Clint turned and looked at the two guards.

"Have either of you seen Matthew Scott in the last couple of hours?"

"No, sir," one said, and the other man shook his head.

"Okay, thanks," Clint said. "You better get back inside."

They went back through the private door, which had been left ajar, and closed it behind them. Clint was left on the outside, which was okay with him. He had better things to do than fight the crowds leaving Madison Square Garden.

One of the things Matthew Scott had written down for him was his own address. It was on the back of the piece of paper with the other four names and addresses. Clint decided that the best way to approach Matthew Scott was head on, so he caught a cab a few blocks away from Madison Square Garden and gave the driver Scott's address.

Scott lived in a building on Tenth Avenue and West Forty-eighth Street, in a section of the city called Hell's Kitchen. Once he got there he saw why. The standard of living there was very poor, with rows and rows of tenements, one of which Matthew Scott apparently lived in. Behind the buildings were railyards and factories, and he saw one sign that indicated that the Manhattan Gas Works was nearby. On the money that P. T. Barnum was paying him, couldn't he have afforded to live somewhere else, somewhere better?

Garbage was piled in front of many of the buildings, and he skirted it as he approached Scott's building. He felt that just by seeing where the young man lived he was learning something about him.

He entered Scott's building and realized that he didn't

know what floor, or what apartment, the man lived in. As he stood there, wondering how to find out, a girl came down a flight of stairs and started to leave the building. She stopped when she saw him. She was dirty, but pretty. Beneath the grime he guessed that she was about eighteen.

"Are you police?" she asked.

"No."

"Interested in a good time?"

"No. I'm looking for someone. Maybe you can help me find him?"

"That depends," she said, coyly.

He took out a dollar and gave it to her. She snatched it from his hand and secreted it somewhere inside her grimy clothes.

"Who ya lookin' for?"

"A man named Matthew Scott."

"Who?"

"He's young, fair-haired, sort of handsome—"

"Oh, you mean Scott."

"Yes, I guess I do."

"He lives in the second floor," she said. "Front apartment."

"Thanks." He started inside, but she stopped him.

"But he ain't there right now."

"Are you sure?"

"Real sure."

"How can you be so sure?"

She smiled and said, "Because I live there, too."

FORTY-EIGHT

Clint decided to buy the girl something to eat. She led him to a small café that was on the fringes of Hell's Kitchen, far enough away so that the waiter gave her a disapproving look.

She said her name was Patty.

"You don't want to have sex?" she asked. "But you wanna buy me somethin' to eat?"

"That's right."

"You must want somethin'."

"Just some information."

"About Scotty?"

"Yes."

She shrugged and said, "Go ahead, ask."

"What's your relationship?"

"He lets me sleep in his place," she said, "and I let him . . . do things when he wants to."

231

"So you're not his girlfriend?"

She laughed and said, "I wouldn't say that." Her laugh revealed teeth that were in tact, but sort of gray. Cleaned up she'd be quite pretty. He had no idea what her body looked like, as her clothes were baggy and loose fitting.

The waiter came with the steak dinner she wanted and she dug in. She used the knife and fork to tear the meat apart rather than cut it, and she picked up the potatoes and carrots with her fingers and stuffed them into her mouth.

"Why didn't you know who I meant when I asked for Matthew Scott?"

"I never knew his whole name," she said. "He just said to call him Scotty."

"Patty, why does he live in that building?"

"I always wondered the same thing," she said. "He's got money, I know that. I mean, he's got nice clothes and all."

"He's never told you?"

"I asked once, and he told me not to ask."

"So you didn't?"

"He told me in a strong way."

"What do you mean?"

"He grabbed me by the hair, put a knife to my throat, and told me not to ask him any questions."

"He's violent?"

"Mister," she said, "he's downright crazy."

"How crazy?"

She looked at him, her face smeared with grease from the steak dinner. He took out two more dollars and put them down on the table. Once again they disappeared into the folds of her clothes.

"I think he kills people."

"Why?'

"Why do I think it, or why does he do it?"

"Let's start with why you think it."

"Because when he was holdin' that knife to my throat I knew he'd kill me in a minute."

"But he didn't."

"I didn't ask him no more questions."

"So then you don't know for sure that he's killed people."

"No."

"But you feel you know that he's capable of it."

"Oh, yes."

"Where are you from, Patty?"

"Here."

"Parents?"

"Dead."

"Any other family?"

"No."

"Would you like to get out of that building?"

"And do what?"

"Live somewhere else."

"Like where?"

"I don't know," he said, "just out of that neighborhood."

She sat back in her chair and seemed to give the question some thought.

"I'm from that neighborhood, Mister," she said, finally. "I wouldn't know what to do anywhere else."

That was the answer he had expected.

"Let me ask you something else, then."

"What?"

"How do you feel about Scotty?"

She shrugged and said, "He gives me a place to sleep."

"And if he didn't?"

"I'd sleep somewhere else."

"Do you have to tell him we had this talk?"

She eyed him slyly and said, "That depends."

"On what? How much?"

She nodded.

"I'll give you ten dollars now," he said, "and ninety before I leave New York if you never tell him about this conversation."

"Fifty now," she said, "fifty later."

"Twenty now," he said, "eighty later. That's as high as I'll go."

"How do I know you'll give me the eighty?"

"Because I don't even have to give you the twenty," he said. "Maybe I kill people, too."

She stared at him, then swallowed and agreed to the twenty-eighty split.

FORTY-NINE

"How much does P. T. pay Matthew Scott?" Clint asked Nancy later that night.

When he got to the house, P. T. was already in bed and would not be up for hours and hours, until the middle of the next day.

"If you wake him," Nancy warned, "he won't be good for anything."

"Then let me ask you the question," Clint said, and did, about Matthew Scott's salary. Both Delvecchio and Sam were looking on.

"I don't know how much he pays Matthew," Nancy said.

"Enough so that he wouldn't have to live in a tenement in Hell's Kitchen?" Clint asked.

"I would think so—why are you picking on Matthew?"

"Because he's in love with you, Nancy," Clint said. "Everybody knows it but you."

She turned to look at Sam, who nodded.

"Also, he lives in Hell's Kitchen, in a rundown tenement with garbage all over the place, and he lives with a young prostitute."

"I can't believe that," Nancy said. "Matthew's a . . . decent man."

"Do you know his background?" Clint asked. "Where he's from?" He'd asked Patty the same thing, but she hadn't known anymore than Nancy did.

"Del," Clint said, "you're the detective. Track that information down for me, will you?"

"What about P. T.?"

"He's in for the night," Clint said. "I'll stay here with Sam."

"Okay, then," Delvecchio said. "I'll see you all tomorrow afternoon."

They all bade him goodnight, and he left.

"You really think Matthew is involved in this?" Nancy asked.

"Nancy," he said, "I already know that he's not what he seems. What we've got to find out now is exactly what he *is*. Have you seen him since the show?"

"No."

"Did you see him there?"

"No," she said. "I was looking after P. T."

"Sam?"

"Didn't see him, Clint."

"Okay," Clint said, "there's nothing I can do about that now. Nancy, just make yourself comfortable, do whatever it is you do after a show."

"I usually have some tea," she said. "Anyone else want some?"

"I'll have some," Sam said. "I'll come and help—"

"No," Nancy said, "that's all right. I can do it myself. Why don't you just stay here and talk to Clint, Sam."

"All right."

Nancy left them alone in the living room.

"Why not go with her?" Clint asked.

"You've got to give your subject some room, Clint," Sam said. "You can't be on them all the time or they'll start resenting you, arguing with you and, eventually, trying to get away from you."

"That makes sense."

"Yes, it does. You think you've got this solved, don't you?"

"I'm still not sure there's even anything to solve, Sam," he said. "I still haven't seen a note, and there haven't been any attempts."

"Some people would say that was good," she pointed out. "No more threats and no attempts? In my business that's a job well done."

"And it may be," Clint said. "I'm not really going to know anything until I know more about Matthew Scott."

"She's amazingly . . . naïve about him."

"Does she have any feelings for him, do you think?"

"Not that I've seen."

"She always seems to . . . ignore him, or not notice that he's there," Clint said. "I thought maybe she was trying too hard."

"That's interesting," Sam said. "I'll have to watch them more closely the next time they're in a room together."

"First we've got to find him," Clint said.

"What about the girl you were talking about?" Sam asked.

"She told me everything she knows."

"Are you sure?"

"I'm sure."

"Then you'll just have to wait until he shows up here."

"Yeah."

"Or until Del finds something out about him."

"Oh, there's plenty to find out about him," Clint said. "This young man is hiding a lot."

"And you think that means he's the one sending threats to Barnum?"

"I think it makes him a good suspect."

"As good as any, I guess."

"What are you thinking, Sam?"

"Just that hiding a past, or the way he lives, doesn't necessarily mean he's our man."

"I agree with that," Clint said. "I guess I just don't like standing around waiting for something to happen."

At that moment there was a knock at the door. They looked at each other and then walked to the door together. She stood off to one side and produced a small gun. Clint didn't see where she'd taken it from. He slid the Colt New Line out from behind his back and palmed it in his left hand, then opened the door with his right. He found himself looking into the face of Lieutenant Gerald Egan.

"Adams," Egan said. "I didn't expect to see you here."

"That makes two of us, Lieutenant," Clint replied. "What can I do for you?"

"I came to see Mr. or Mrs. Barnum."

"About what?"

"I think I'll talk to them about what."

"Mr. Barnum isn't available," Clint said. "I'll get Mrs. Barnum for you."

"Can I come in?"

"No," Clint said, "I'll get Mrs. Barnum for you, though. Just wait there."

"Now wait a minute—" Egan said, but Clint closed the door in his face.

"Why won't you let him in?" Sam asked. "He's a policeman."

"I don't trust him," Clint said. "Why don't you get Nancy and bring her here. Then we can find out what he wants."

"Okay."

Clint waited until Sam returned with Nancy, who was looking concerned.

"What does he want?" she asked.

"That's what you're going to find out," Clint said.

"Shall I let him in?"

"That's up to you."

"What about me?" Sam asked.

"Move into the hallway behind the stairs," Clint said. "You'll be able to hear and see from there."

"All right."

Sam moved, Clint nodded and Nancy opened the door.

"Mrs. Barnum?" Egan asked.

"That's right."

Egan looked behind her at Clint.

"Can I help you?" Nancy asked.

"I'd like to speak to you—in private."

"Mr. Adams can hear whatever you have to say to me."

"Well, can I come in, at least?"

Nancy seemed to think it over, then said, "All right."

She stepped back to allow Egan to enter. She and Clint led him into the living room. Sam came out from behind the stairs and moved to the living room door so she could hear.

"Is Mr. Barnum available, Ma'am?" Egan asked.

"No, he's not," she said. "I understood that you asked to see either of us."

"Yeah, that's right," he said, "you'll do."

"Then what is it?" she asked. "What can I do for you?"

"When's the last time you saw Matthew Scott?"

"Matthew?"

"You do know him, don't you?"

"Well, yes. He works for my husband."

"When did you see him last."

"Sometime today, I think."

"When?"

"This morning."

"Not since?"

"No, not since."

Egan looked at Clint.

"You know him?"

"We've been introduced."

"When did you see him last?"

"Yesterday, I think. What's this all about, Lieutenant?"

"We found Matthew Scott this morning, in an alley in Hell's Kitchen," Egan said. "He'd been shot."

Nancy caught her breath.

"Is he all right?"

"No, Ma'am, he's not," Egan said. "Fact of the matter is, he's dead."

FIFTY

Nancy sat down heavily on a nearby chair.

"When was he found?" Clint asked.

"This afternoon."

"How late?"

"I don't know, Adams," Egan said. "He's dead, that's what I came to tell Mrs. Barnum." He looked at her. "Also to ask if you knew anyone who might have wanted him dead."

She looked up at him, her face pale, and said, "No."

"You?" he asked Clint.

"No."

"What was his job?"

"He was my husband's assistant."

"Where were you and your husband this afternoon?"

"At Madison Square Garden," she said.

"Anyone see you?"

"Lots of people."

"I saw them."

Egan looked at Clint.

"And who saw you?"

"I did," Nancy said.

"That's cozy," the lieutenant said. "You alibi each other."

"Ask the security guards at the Garden, Lieutenant," Clint suggested. "They'll tell you."

"I'll do that," Egan said.

"Is that all?" Clint asked.

"For now."

"I'll walk the lieutenant to the door," Clint told Nancy.

She nodded. Clint and Egan left the room and walked to the front door together.

"She looked pretty shook up," Egan said.

"She is."

"What was her relationship with Scott?"

"He worked for her husband."

"That's all?"

"That's all," Clint said, opening the front door. "What else did you expect?"

"Well," he said, "she's a lot younger than her husband, and Scott was a good-looking young man her age. I thought maybe—"

"You thought wrong."

"You sure?"

"I'm sure."

"Sounds like you been doin' some of my job for me, Adams."

"I don't think so, Lieutenant," Clint said, and closed the door.

Sam came out from behind the stairs and approached Clint.

"Wow," she said. "There goes our number-one suspect. I guess Del's wasting his time now."

"Not necessarily," Clint said. "Maybe Scott was working with somebody. Maybe Delvecchio will come up with a name."

"Maybe," Sam said. "I better go and check on Nancy, see if she's all right."

"Okay."

"What are you gonna do?"

"Nothing, I guess," he said. "I'm stuck here, and Matthew Scott is dead. I guess I'll have to start all over in the morning."

"I'll show you where Del was sleeping," she said, "later."

"Okay."

She nodded and went into the living room. Clint wondered if Patty knew that Scott was dead. He wondered exactly when the young man had been killed. Hadn't somebody said they saw him at the Garden that day? Who had it been? Had he left the Garden before or during the show? And did this exonerate him of any involvement in the threats to P. T. and Nancy Barnum?

He only knew the answer to the last question: no.

FIFTY-ONE

Nancy Barnum prepared a dinner for Clint, Sam and herself, but barely ate anything. Afterward, she excused herself and said she would see them in the morning. She said that Sam could show Clint where to sleep.

When she was gone, Clint helped Sam clear the dishes and clean up, and then they went into the living room and had some brandy.

"I've been thinking about it," she said.

"About what?"

"The murder of Matthew Scott and what it means."

"It means he's dead," Clint said.

"Yes, but it doesn't necessarily mean that he wasn't involved in the original threats," she said. "Maybe he was and had a falling out with a partner or an employer."

"That's possible," Clint said. "That leaves us to still discover who that partner or employer was. What it does do, however, is make the list he gave me suspect. I'll have to start over again."

"And get a list from who this time?"

"I don't know," he said. "Maybe Nancy."

"Nancy doesn't seem to think anyone would want to hurt her husband."

Clint paused a moment and then said, "Maybe the answer is somewhere in the house."

"Like where? And what?"

"I don't know," Clint said, "but the last time I saw Scott, he was searching through the office at Madison Square Garden."

"For what?"

"He wouldn't say."

"So you think he was looking for something that has some bearing on what's going on?"

"I can't be sure," Clint said. "All I know is that he was looking for *something*."

"So if he didn't find it, maybe it's in this house somewhere."

"Maybe in his office."

They both put down their brandy glasses, got up and walked to Barnum's office together.

"You check the desk," Clint said.

"What are we looking for?"

"I don't know," he answered. "I guess maybe we'll know when we find it."

She walked to the desk and started going through the drawers. Clint began looking on the bookshelves and in file cabinets. After two hours of searching they both stopped and stared at each other.

"Whatever it is," he said, "it's either not here or we're not seeing it."

"What do we do now?"

"I guess we'd better turn in, too," he said. "There's not much else we can do. Why don't you show me to my room."

"All right."

They went to the second floor together, and Sam walked him down the hall to his room.

"I'm just across the hall," she said. "Should we take turns?"

"I don't think so," he said. "I'll go around the house once to check that all the doors and windows are secure, and then we can just both go to sleep. After all, we still have no proof anyone is going to try to hurt P. T."

"Scott's death doesn't prove that?"

"No," he said, "that only proves that somebody wanted to hurt him."

"I wonder why?"

"Tomorrow," he said, "after Del comes back, I'll go to where Scott lived and look around. Maybe there's something there that will give us some answers."

"All right," Sam said. "I guess I'll go to bed then."

"Good night," he said. "See you in the morning."

" 'Night."

He watched as she went into her room and closed the door behind her and then went downstairs to check the doors and windows.

FIFTY-TWO

Delvecchio showed up earlier in the morning than Clint expected. He heard someone knocking, and then banging, on the front door. He sat up in bed, looked down at the naked form next to him. He wasn't sure when she had come into his bed, but he certainly could recall the energy and passion she had brought with her.

She opened her eyes suddenly and asked, "What is it?"

"Somebody's at the door," he said. "I'll get it."

He got up, pulled on his pants, and grabbed his gun, and ran down the stairs to the door. He opened it, gun at the ready, then relaxed when he saw Delvecchio.

"We got stuff to talk about," the detective said. "Oh, did I wake you?"

"What time is it?"

"Eight AM"

"Yeah, you woke me."

"What about the others?"

Clint hesitated, then said, "I think the women are still asleep. I'll check. Why don't you wait in the living room."

"All right, but hurry. I've got big news."

"I'll be right back."

Clint went up and found Nancy waiting in the hallway.

"What is it?"

"It's Delvecchio," Clint said. "He's got some news."

"I'll get dressed and come down."

"That's all right," Clint said. "I'll find out what he's learned and fill you in."

"Then I better check on P. T."

She turned and went to her husband's room. Clint went back into his room and looked at Sam, who was sitting up in bed. He remembered, now. She had come to his room soon after he'd turned in, slipping in quietly, probably thinking he was asleep. As she joined him in the bed he became aware of the fact that she was naked. The heat her body gave off was intense, and when he reached for her, her breasts filled his hands to overflowing. They had gone at each other with a quiet hunger and desperation, not wanting Nancy or P. T. to hear them.

"What is it?" she asked.

"Get dressed," he said. "Delvecchio's back and he's got news."

She got out of bed and started to dress hurriedly. He would like to have watched her, but instead he got dressed himself. When they went back downstairs, there was no indication that they had spent the night together—and yet Delvecchio gave them a somewhat knowing look.

"First," Clint said, "we should tell you that the police were here last night. Lieutenant Egan."

"What'd he want?"

"To tell us that Matthew Scott is dead."

"What?"

"Somebody shot him."

"Jesus," Delvecchio said, "and I thought that what I found out pointed to him as our man—or at least that he was part of it."

"What did you find out?" Clint asked.

"You want the long or the short version?"

"I want to know what you found out," Clint said. "How you did it is your business. I assume you have a lot of contacts in lots of places in this city. Just tell us what it is."

"You're gonna like this."

Clint stared at him.

"Matthew Scott's real name is Matthew Forepaugh."

"Adam Forepaugh's son?" Clint asked.

"Son or nephew, I guess," Delvecchio said, "I'm not sure. But definitely a relative."

"Damn!" Clint said. Had Forepaugh been lying to him, and lying so well?

"Forepaugh could have planted him with Barnum long ago," Clint said.

"Or maybe they weren't working together at all," Sam said. "Maybe this is just a coincidence. Maybe he worked for Barnum because he didn't want to work for a relative."

"Clint doesn't like coincidences," Delvecchio said. "He doesn't believe in them."

"And this would be too much of one," Clint said.

"So what do we do now?" she asked.

"I'm still going to go and take a look at where Scott lived," Clint said, "and then I suppose I'll have to go and talk to Forepaugh again."

"Even if Forepaugh did plant Matthew with Barnum," Delvecchio said, "what was the purpose? And who killed Matthew?"

"Questions I'm going to try to find the answers to," Clint said.

At that moment, Nancy Barnum came down, wearing a floor-length robe. She had her arms folded in front of her, as if she were hugging herself against the cold.

"What's going on?" she asked.

"I've got to get dressed to go out," Clint said. "Sam, can you fill Nancy in on what we know?"

"Of course."

Sam drew Nancy aside and began to talk to her.

"Am I back inside?" Delvecchio asked.

"Yes," Clint said, "and so is Barnum, until after I talk to Forepaugh. Now that Scott has been killed, we'll have to keep P. T. inside."

"Can we do that?" Delvecchio asked. "I mean, will he let us?"

"Maybe, with Nancy's help," Clint said. "Let me get dressed, and then I'll talk to her about it. This was good work, Del."

Delvecchio shrugged and said, "It's what I do. Are you sure you don't want to know the particulars?"

"No time," Clint said. As he went upstairs, Delvecchio looked disappointed.

FIFTY-THREE

Clint got to Scott's building in Hell's Kitchen in time to catch Patty before she left. He banged on the door until she answered it, rubbing the sleep from her eyes.

"Back already?" she asked. "I ain't seen him since we talked." Then her eyes cleared and she looked at him anxiously. "You bring the rest of my money?"

"I've got some bad news, Patty."

"You ain't payin' me?"

"I'll pay you," he said. "Let me come in."

"Sure, why not?" she said. "Like I said, Scotty ain't here. Don't know where he is."

Clint entered and closed the door. The place was sparsely furnished and in need of a good cleaning, which he doubted it would get from Patty.

"So what's the bad news?"

"Scott's not coming back, Patty," Clint said. "He's dead."

"Whataya mean, dead?"

"I mean somebody killed him. Shot him."

"Sonofabitch," she said. "So I guess this place is mine until somebody kicks me out."

"You're not upset?"

"Why should I be?" she asked. "I already tol' you I ain't his girlfriend. So he's dead. I just got to find somebody else to get a free ride off of for a while. Hey, does this mean I don't get the rest of my money?"

Clint took out eighty dollars and handed it to her. She waved it in front of her face, closing her eyes to either the scent or the breeze.

"You sure you don't want somethin' back for it?"

"Actually, yes, I do."

"I thought so," she said. She started to take off her top, but he stopped her.

"No, not that," he said. "I just want to take a look around."

"That's all?"

"That's it."

"Be my guest. You mind if I go back to sleep?"

"Go ahead. I'll try not to bother you."

"You'll let yerself out?"

"Yes."

She yawned and said, "You better look in here first so you don't wake me up later."

He followed her into a small bedroom. The apartment was three rooms, all small, all filthy. The sheets on the bed were soiled. Clint guessed that Patty slept there most of the time, but not Matthew Scott—who was actually Matthew Forepaugh. In fact, Clint guessed that Matthew had someplace else to sleep entirely. He had probably only taken this place to go with the Matthew "Scott" name.

"What are you lookin' for?"

"I don't know."

She threw herself down on the bed, still holding the money.

"Then how you gonna know when you find it?"

"Don't know that either."

She rolled over, money clutched in her hand, and said, "I'm too tired to figure out what that means."

To Clint's utter surprise, she was asleep the next moment.

Clint searched the place from top to bottom, but not knowing what you're looking for is a definite disadvantage. He finished and slipped out without waking Patty again. He was preoccupied as he went down the stairs, figuring that his next move had to be to talk to Adam Forepaugh again. Actually, his next move turned out to be talking to Lieutenant Egan again because Egan was standing outside as Clint came out.

"Well, well, Adams," Egan said. "And what brings you to a dead man's home in the middle of the afternoon?"

"I'm here on behalf of the Barnums," Clint said without hesitation. "They wanted to see if Scott had taken home any of their papers."

"And did he?"

"Not that I can find."

"That's good," Egan said. "You don't mind if I check your pockets, do you? To see if you removed anything?"

"Be my guest."

Egan did such a poor job of searching Clint that he

missed the Colt New Line tucked into his belt at the small of his back.

"I guess you didn't take anything out," Egan admitted, grudgingly.

"What brings you here, Lieutenant?"

"Trying to do my job and find a killer, that's what. Why don't you go on your way and stay out of mine, huh?"

"My pleasure, Egan," Clint said. "I'm going to do my best not to ever see you again."

"That would suit me just fine."

Clint gave Egan a mock salute and walked off down the street. He waited until he was a few blocks away before waving down a passing horse-drawn cab and giving the driver Adam Forepaugh's address.

The killer looked at the man seated behind the desk.

"He was getting in my way," he said.

"You didn't have to kill him."

"I did have to," the standing man said, "and now with him removed, I can go after Barnum."

"I don't want P. T. Barnum dead," the seated man said. "I thought I made that clear."

"Well then, young Matthew had his own agenda, didn't he?" the killer asked. "Because he told me that Barnum's death was the ultimate goal."

The man behind the desk rubbed his hands over his face, then removed them when he heard a knock at the front door.

"Step into the other room," he said, quickly. "I don't want anyone to see you."

"You're the boss," the killer said, "or, anyway, the man with the money."

"That's right," the seated man said, "I am, and if you want to get some more of my money, you'll do exactly as I say."

"Oh, I will," the killer said, and then added to himself, "for now."

FIFTY-FOUR

Delvecchio decided he'd better talk to P. T. Barnum.

"He'll be up soon," Nancy said.

"Is there any way to get him up sooner?" Delvecchio asked.

"Why?"

"I get the feeling Clint might be walking into something," the detective said, "and it's on your behalf."

"What do you want to talk to him about?" she asked.

"Matthew Scott," Delvecchio said, "that is, Matthew Forepaugh."

"I can't believe that Matthew is—was—related to Adam Forepaugh."

"That's what my information indicates," Delvecchio said, "and it comes from a reliable source."

"What source?"

"A lawyer," Delvecchio said. "A lawyer who used to

work for Adam Forepaugh but was fired."

"So maybe he's just out for revenge and is giving you bad information?" Sam asked.

Delvecchio looked at her and asked, "Why is it you're always playing devil's advocate?"

She smiled and said, "Because I'm good at it."

"Well," Delvecchio said, "not this time. This is a reputable lawyer who is not looking for revenge. In fact, he wasn't offering any information. Apparently, he was just waiting for someone to ask him the right questions."

"Which you did?" Sam asked.

"Apparently."

"I'll go up and see if P. T. is stirring," she said. "Sometimes I can get him up before he's ready."

Nancy left the living room and went upstairs.

"What do you think Clint is walking into?" Sam asked.

"I'm not sure," Delvecchio said. "I just have a bad feeling."

"Do you think he's the one in danger now," she asked, "and not the Barnums?"

"You mean do I think we should leave here and go after him?" Delvecchio answered. "No, not quite yet . . . well, maybe one of us."

Forepaugh's manservant showed Clint into the man's office. He was sitting behind his desk, looking harried.

"Mr. Adams," Forepaugh said, "Back again?"

"I have more questions, Mr. Forepaugh?"

"About P. T. Barnum?"

"Sort of," Clint said. "It's about a young man who works for Barnum. His name is Matthew Scott."

Forepaugh's eyes shifted enough to tell Clint he was

on the right track. The name meant something to Forepaugh, all right.

"What about him?"

"Do you know him?"

"I've met Mr. Scott in my dealings with P. T., yes."

"Then you'll be sad to know the young man is dead."

"That is distressing news."

It was evident that Forepaugh already knew that Scott was dead, because he never registered any surprise.

"Even more distressing for you," Clint said, "since he was related to you, wasn't he?"

Forepaugh didn't answer.

"Same last name," Clint said. "That would make him either a nephew . . . or a son?"

Forepaugh firmed his jaw, and for a moment Clint didn't think he was going to get an answer. Then he said, "Yes, he was my son."

FIFTY-FIVE

"How many?" Clint asked.

"Two," Forepaugh said, "two sons, each with a different mother, each with a different personality . . . and each with the same goal."

"Which was?"

"P. T. Barnum's money and reputation."

"And how did they expect to get that?"

"One by exposing him as a phony, thereby assuring me of gaining from Barnum's disgrace, and then gaining when it came time for him to inherit."

"Or so he thought."

"Yes."

That would have been Matthew "Scott," and would explain why he was searching for something in Barnum's office.

"And the other?"

"By killing Barnum."

"He's the one sending the threats?"

"Yes."

"Why? Why not just kill him?"

"He thought Barnum was old and feeble enough to die of fright, I suppose," Forepaugh said.

"And what happens when he realizes he can't scare him to death?"

Forepaugh spread his hands helplessly and said, "I suppose he'd kill him."

"And what about Matthew?" Clint asked. "Do you know who killed him?"

"I'm afraid it was his . . . half brother," Forepaugh said.

"But why?"

"Because he was getting in his way."

"How?"

"Well, for one, by bringing you in to protect Barnum."

"So he killed his own brother?"

"You have to realize," Forepaugh said, "that these two boys never knew each other until they happened to find me around the same time. It was just a coincidence."

Clint flinched at the word.

"So it wasn't really like he was killing his brother," Forepaugh said.

"Or your son?" Clint asked. "Tell me, Forepaugh, do you look at either of these boys as a son?"

"I felt a . . . responsibility to them," Forepaugh said, "but no, I can't say that I ever thought of them as sons."

"So was either of them really going to inherit everything from you?"

"Not everything," Forepaugh said, "but enough."

"Enough to kill you for?"

"What?" Forepaugh looked shocked.

"If one of them wanted his inheritance enough to kill Barnum, why not kill you, too?" Clint asked. "After all, if you didn't feel that they were your sons, what makes you think they thought of you as a father?"

Forepaugh considered this for a moment, then his eyes went to a door in the wall on the right.

"Is he in there?" Clint asked, lowering his voice. "Is that another room?"

"Yes," Forepaugh said, to both questions.

Clint drew his gun and approached the door. He put his hand on the doorknob, turning it gently, then pushed the door open and dove into the room. He felt silly when the room turned out to be empty. In the back was another door.

"Where does that lead?" Clint asked Forepaugh.

"To a hallway, and out."

"Could he have heard our entire conversation?"

"From that room, yes."

"Then he heard you say you didn't think of him as a son."

"W-what do you think he'll do?"

"I think he's going to go after Barnum," Clint said, "and then come after you."

"You have to stop him."

"I don't know his name or what he looks like."

"His name," Forepaugh said, "is Victor Alonzo."

"Not Forepaugh?"

"He didn't take my name the way Matthew did. He kept his mother's name."

"What's he looks like?"

"Tall, dark hair, dark skin—nothing like Matthew. Their mothers were very different."

"Has he been around?" Clint asked. "Have I seen him?"

"He did not infiltrate P. T.'s life the way Matthew did. He didn't think it necessary, and he did not have the patience for it."

"But he had the patience to send threatening letters." Clint wasn't sure he was buying Forepaugh's entire explanation. Maybe, after all, the threats *were* the work of Adam Forepaugh. Maybe he was more in control of his sons than he let on—until now. (Until one had killed the other, gone completely *out* of control.)

"I have to get back," Clint said, and left Forepaugh's office before the man could say another word.

Delvecchio was approaching the front door of Adam Forepaugh's house when it opened and Clint came rushing out.

"What are you doing here?" Clint demanded.

"I came to help—"

"Who's at the house? Just Sam?"

"Yes, why?"

"Let's go," Clint said, grabbing the detective's arm. "I'll explain on the way."

FIFTY-SIX

Samantha Sharpe answered the knock at the door with her gun held low in her left hand, down by her leg. If she'd been holding it anywhere else she would have had a better chance of stopping the man from entering the house. When she cracked the door open, the man immediately hit it with his shoulder. The door struck her left arm first, striking the protruding bone in her wrist, causing her to drop the gun. The door then drove her back with such force that she landed on her back. By the time she managed to sit up, the man was inside, the door was closed and he was pointing a gun at her.

"Where are they?" he asked. He was a tall man with dark hair, dark eyes and dark skin. She'd never see him before and yet, there was something vaguely familiar about him.

"Where's who?"

"Don't play with me, lady," the man said. "I'm in no mood. Where is Barnum and his wife?"

"Sam," a woman's voice called from upstairs, "who was that at the door?"

"Nancy! Stay upstairs!" Sam called. "Don't come down!"

The man cocked the hammer on his gun and jabbed it toward Sam.

"Is he upstairs, too?"

"Mister," Sam said, "you don't want to do this. You don't—"

"Don't tell me what I want!" the man said. "I know what I want. Get up. We're going upstairs."

Sam got to her feet and said, "I can't let you do that. I can't let you go upstairs."

"How're you gonna stop me?" he demanded.

Sam looked over at her gun, which was on the floor in the middle of the entry foyer. The man with the gun in his hand looked over there as well. He flexed his hand on the butt of his gun and shuffled his feet nervously.

"Don't think about it," he said. "You'll never make it."

"What's your name?" Sam asked.

"What?"

"Your name?"

"Victor Alonzo," he said. It had been Sam's experience that when you asked somebody their name, no matter what the situation, they tended to answer.

"Victor, have you ever killed anyone before?"

"What do you care?"

"I care," she said, "because I don't want to be the first."

"Well, don't you worry," he said, his eye flicking up

the stairs, "if you're the first, you won't be the last."

"You want to kill P. T. Barnum, is that it?"

"That's right."

"Why?" she asked. "Why do you want to do that, Victor?"

"Never mind," Victor said. "Just—let's go upstairs."

"I have to go for that gun on the floor, Victor," she said. "That's my job."

"If you do that," he said, "I'll have to kill you."

"Well," she said, "you have to do what you have to do, and I have to do what I have to do."

"Please," Victor said, "don't . . ."

When Clint and Delvecchio reached the Barnum house, Clint said to the detective, "You go around the back."

"How do we know he's in there?"

"We have to assume it," Clint said. "Now go!"

Delvecchio disappeared behind the house on the run and Clint started for the front door. That was when he heard the shot. He drew his gun and crashed into the door.

"Damn!" Sam thought as the bullet struck her. She'd calculated wrong. She wasn't fast enough and Victor Alonzo *would* shoot.

The door slammed open and Clint Adams came rushing in.

"There!" Sam shouted, pointing up the stairs.

Clint looked up the stairs. Victor Alonzo had reached the top of the stairs and now turned. He saw Clint Adams, pointed his gun and shouted, "No! Go away!"

Clint fired once. The bullet struck Alonzo in the chest. He staggered and dropped his gun. It tumbled end over end down the steps and then he fell forward and followed it. His tumbling came to a stop right at Clint's feet. Clint bent over to check the man to make sure he was dead. Delvecchio arrived on the scene from somewhere in the back, and they both rushed to Sam.

"Where are you hit?" Clint asked.

"I'm ashamed to say."

Clint and Delvecchio rolled her over and saw the bullet wound on her right buttock.

"We'll get you to a doctor," Delvecchio said, "and maybe he can save your ass."

EPILOGUE

Clint entered P. T. Barnum's office two days later. The old showman was seated behind his desk.

"Thank you for coming," Barnum said. "How much longer will you be in New York?"

"I'm leaving tomorrow."

"Have a seat," Barnum said. It was on toward evening, when Barnum's energy level was approaching its highest. His eyes were bright and alive. He was almost the Barnum Clint remembered meeting in 1870.

"I'm sorry about Matthew, P. T.," Clint said. "He didn't turn out to be who you thought he was."

"Thank you," Barnum said, "that *was* a disappointment. I thought that young man would succeed me. Never had any sons, you know."

"I know."

"And to find out that he was Forepaugh's son—I

never knew Adam had a son, let alone two."

"He didn't know, either, until it was too late," Clint said. "They both turned out a little twisted because of that—one more than the other."

"I suppose I should feel sorry for Adam," Barnum said.

"That's debatable."

"What do you mean?"

"I'm not sure he wasn't behind this whole thing, P. T.," Clint said. "I can't prove it, though. I'd be real careful if I were you."

"For the rest if my life? Not that that'll be too much longer."

"Keep Delvecchio around."

"Maybe I'll do that," Barnum said. "Right now, I want to thank you. You saved my life, but more importantly you saved Nancy's."

"Samantha Sharpe did that," Clint said. "She kept talking to him, kept him downstairs, kept him there until we could get here—and took a bullet doing it."

"I know," Barnum said. "I'm taking care of all her medical bills, and I'm doubling everyone's fee."

"Not mine," Clint said. "I did it as a favor. Give whatever you were going to give me to them."

"Fine," Barnum said, "but I still want to do something for you."

"That's okay, P. T.—"

"What about my offer?" P. T. asked. "I don't have much time left, Clint. We could make a lot of money together."

"P. T.," Clint said, "I'm sorry, but . . . I'm just not a white elephant."

Barnum studied Clint and said, "All right, I can see

that. But I still want to do something for you."

"P. T.—"

"Help me up," Barnum said. "We have to go some-place."

"P. T.—"

"Come on, come on," Barnum said, getting unsteadily to his feet, "while I still have the energy . . ."

They got Barnum's driver to bring the buggy around and Barnum told the driver to take them to the Garden.

"I really don't want to see the circus tonight, P. T.," Clint said.

"That's good," Barnum said, "because there is no show tonight."

"Why are we going to Madison Square Garden, then?"

"You'll see," Barnum said, "you'll see . . ."

Upon arrival at the Garden, Barnum had the buggy drop them behind the structure. They got out and Clint walked in with Barnum on his arm. Clint found himself in the back where they kept Jumbo and the other animals.

"P. T.," Clint said, "what are we doing here?"

"You'll see," the showman said, mysteriously, "you'll see. Have some patience."

They walked at Barnum's pace, so it seemed to take forever to get wherever they were going. Finally, they entered a stable where the horses were kept.

Barnum stopped and pointed to a stall.

"There."

"What's there?" Clint asked, puzzled.

"Go and see."

Clint moved away from Barnum, who stood steadily

on his own, no longer supported. Clint looked into the
stall and saw a magnificent horse, standing more than
sixteen hands high. Its neck was longer and lighter than
that of others he had seen. It was facing out, and its eyes
were wide-set and intelligent. The animal was well-
muscled and had long legs with pronounced tendons. It
was a powerful animal to say the least. And the coat was
black, blacker than he had ever seen, blacker even than
the black of his beloved Duke. The black of night with
no hint of light. But right between the animal's eyes was
a sliver of white, a crescent shape, like a tiny sliver of
light showing behind an eclipse.

"What is this?" Clint asked Barnum. He did so without turning, for he could not take his eyes from the animal.

"He's yours," Barnum said. "He's three years old, so
he has some growing to do, yet. He's a thoroughbred
from England, a Darley Arabian, best of the three foun-
dation thoroughbred stallions. He is also a direct de-
scendant of the great Eclipse, who was undefeated in
eighteen races, or so they tell me. What's the great de-
scription of one of his victories? Oh yes, 'Eclipse first,
the rest nowhere.' "

Clint turned to face Barnum, a question in his eyes.

"I understand you've been looking for a replacement
for your wonderful gelding, the one who made you
change your mind about ever getting close to a horse
again."

"Yes, but—"

"I can't replace Duke, not completely, but this is the
finest animal I've ever seen, which is why I brought him
here from Europe. I was going to use him in the show

business, but now he's yours. This is my gratitude to you, Clint, for the life of my Nancy. You can't refuse."

"P. T.—"

"You can't!"

Clint turned and looked at the horse again, and the animal seemed to be looking back at him. He moved closer and put out his hand. The Darley Arabian sniffed it, nuzzled it, then allowed him to pet it.

"This undefeated Eclipse," Clint said. "When did he live?"

"He was foaled in seventeen hundred, I believe," Barnum said.

"Then is there any reason why I couldn't name this one Eclipse?"

"None that I could see," Barnum said. "After all, he's your horse."

Clint walked around the animal, inspecting its withers, its shoulders, its girth. He ran his hands up and down its legs and hip, walked all the way around until he was facing the animal again. He knew he had finally found, or been given, the horse he'd been looking for during the months since he'd put Duke out to pasture.

"Eclipse it is, then," he said, turning to Barnum, "and I accept him with thanks."

"I hope you have as successful a partnership with him as you had for years with your Duke."

Suddenly, Barnum staggered and would have fallen if Clint had not rushed to his side to support him.

"Take me back home, Clint," Barnum said, "and then be on your way. We won't meet again, I fear, but something positive has come from our second meeting, unlike our first."

"Yes," Clint said, "yes, P. T., it has."

Barnum looked at him and said, "I wasn't just talking about the horse."

"Neither was I," Clint said.

Watch for

WANTED: CLINT ADAMS

226th novel in the exciting GUNSMITH series
from Jove

Coming in October!

J. R. ROBERTS
THE GUNSMITH

JAKE LOGAN
TODAY'S HOTTEST ACTION WESTERN!

☐ SLOCUM AND THE WOLF HUNT #237	0-515-12413-3/$4.99
☐ SLOCUM AND THE BARONESS #238	0-515-12436-2/$4.99
☐ SLOCUM AND THE COMANCHE PRINCESS #239	0-515-12449-4/$4.99
☐ SLOCUM AND THE LIVE OAK BOYS #240	0-515-12467-2/$4.99
☐ SLOCUM #241: SLOCUM AND THE BIG THREE	0-515-12484-2/$4.99
☐ SLOCUM #242: SLOCUM AT SCORPION BEND	0-515-12510-5/$4.99
☐ SLOCUM AND THE BUFFALO HUNTER #243	0-515-12518-0/$4.99
☐ SLOCUM AND THE YELLOW ROSE OF TEXAS #244	0-515-12532-6/$4.99
☐ SLOCUM AND THE LADY FROM ABILINE #245	0-515-12555-5/$4.99
☐ SLOCUM GIANT: SLOCUM AND THE THREE WIVES	0-515-12569-5/$5.99
☐ SLOCUM AND THE CATTLE KING #246	0-515-12571-7/$4.99
☐ SLOCUM #247: DEAD MAN'S SPURS	0-515-12613-6/$4.99
☐ SLOCUM #248: SHOWDOWN AT SHILOH	0-515-12659-4/$4.99
☐ SLOCUM AND THE KETCHEM GANG #249	0-515-12686-1/$4.99
☐ SLOCUM AND THE JERSEY LILY #250	0-515-12706-X/$4.99
☐ SLOCUM AND THE GAMBLER'S WOMAN #251	0-515-12733-7/$4.99
☐ SLOCUM AND THE GUNRUNNERS #252	0-515-12754-X/$4.99
☐ SLOCUM AND THE NEBRASKA STORM #253	0-515-12769-8/$4.99
☐ SLOCUM #254: SLOCUM'S CLOSE CALL	0-515-12789-2/$4.99
☐ SLOCUM AND THE UNDERTAKER #255	0-515-12807-4/$4.99
☐ SLOCUM AND THE POMO CHIEF #256	0-515-12838-4/$4.99

Prices slightly higher in Canada

Payable by Visa, MC or AMEX only ($10.00 min.), No cash, checks or COD. Shipping & handling:
US/Can. $2.75 for one book, $1.00 for each add'l book; Int'l $5.00 for one book, $1.00 for each
add'l. Call (800) 788-6262 or (201) 933-9292, fax (201) 896-8569 or mail your orders to:
#(12/99)

Penguin Putnam Inc.	Bill my: ☐ Visa ☐ MasterCard ☐ Amex _____ (expires)
P.O. Box 12289, Dept. B	Card# _____
Newark, NJ 07101-5289	
Please allow 4-6 weeks for delivery.	Signature _____
Foreign and Canadian delivery 6-8 weeks.	

Bill to:

Name _____

Address _____ City _____

State/ZIP _____ Daytime Phone # _____

Ship to:

Name _____	Book Total	$ _____
Address _____	Applicable Sales Tax	$ _____
City _____	Postage & Handling	$ _____
State/ZIP _____	Total Amount Due	$ _____

This offer subject to change without notice. Ad # 202 (4/00)

LONGARM

Explore the exciting Old West with one of the men who made it wild!